Ridgeway's Bride

Cassie Edmond was puzzled by the odd behaviour of those around her. First it was the curious bark from their dog Butte, then the old Ute called Charlie who sometimes called to trade for coffee and flour but now sat silent on his droop-headed paint at the yard gate. Finally it was her father, lifting down his Winchester to go hunting for meat when the meal she'd been preparing was ready for the table.

But when Brad Edmond returned home, carried by Charlie Ute and a stranger, his life slipping away, his back shredded by shotgun pellets, it was the start of a night of unexpected violence for Cassie, and days of trouble for the stranger Walt Ridgeway.

Ridgeway's Bride

Will DuRey

A Black Horse Western

ROBERT HALE

© Will DuRey 2019
First published in Great Britain 2019

ISBN 978-0-7198-3013-6

The Crowood Press
The Stable Block
Crowood Lane
Ramsbury
Marlborough
Wiltshire SN8 2HR

www.bhwesterns.com

Robert Hale is an imprint
of The Crowood Press

The right of Will DuRey to be identified as
author of this work has been asserted by him
in accordance with the Copyright, Designs and
Patents Act 1988

Typeset by
Derek Doyle & Associates, Shaw Heath
Printed and bound in Great Britain by
4Bind Ltd, Stevenage, SG1 2XT

ONE

Outside the dog barked, not the repeated welcoming yelps for a recognized visitor, nor the low throat grumble raised by the scent of an encroaching natural enemy, wolf, bear or snake, but a single sharp sound that registered Butte's surprise, his need for assistance to resolve a puzzling situation.

Cassie crossed the room to look out the window. Across the yard, at the gateway thirty yards distant, a lone rider sat motionless in the saddle. He was scrawny, his body barely filling the red wool shirt and cross-belted dungarees he wore. His faded brown hat was misshapen, weathered by years of constant use, and the expression on his long face was that of a man whose past had known few pleasures. And the droop-headed paint he rode seemed no less weary with life. No one knew the rider's real name, but because of his tribal ancestry he was known as Charlie Ute. He lived alone in a cabin that had been deserted by unlucky gold-seekers on the far side of Eagle Pass.

Charlie wasn't a stranger to Cassie – he'd been an

occasional visitor to her home since she was a child, usually when he needed coffee or flour or some other store-bought commodity that he preferred to barter for with the outlying settlers rather than attempt to trade with Basil Deepcut who ran the emporium in Elkhill. Deepcut never attempted to disguise his disdain for Charlie, and the Ute was sure that he was cheated in every transaction. The store owner's attitude was akin to most of the other towns-people, which made the township an uncomfortable place for Charlie to visit. In the past, he'd suffered random acts of violence at the hands of men bored with pushing cattle, fired up with whiskey, or simply content in the knowledge that the assault wouldn't attract any retribution from the law.

Cassie wondered why Charlie hadn't ridden right up to the house, as was his custom. His stopping at the gate had confused Butte, but the dog was now happily padding across the yard at her father's heels, content that his warning bark had brought an instant response. When her father engaged in conversation with Charlie, Cassie returned to her interrupted chore, only vaguely aware that Charlie had brought neither game nor pelts with which to trade.

A few minutes later, when her father opened the door, Cassie asked if Charlie had gone.

'Not yet.'

'Should I put a plate on the table for him?' Like her mother before her, Cassie always invited Charlie to eat with them if his visit coincided with meal-time, and this evening, with their drovers currently out at the line cabin, there was plenty in the pot. Once or twice Charlie had stayed, but mostly he didn't linger after striking a bargain with her father for the goods he needed. Cassie didn't know if his reluctance was due to a mistrust of their motives, embarrassment because he hadn't mastered the use of knife and fork, or simply because he didn't like her cooking, but he was a silent, watchful guest, and quick to depart when the meal was over.

'I'll ask him when we return,' her father said, his thoughts clearly focused on some other matter.

'Where are you going?' she asked. 'I was about to serve up dinner.'

'It'll keep, won't it? We shouldn't be long. Charlie saw some men down at the stream. I need to find out what they're up to.'

'Who are they?'

'I'm not sure,' he said.

Brad Edmond didn't often lie to his daughter, but he didn't want to worry her by revealing that Charlie had recognized the group as men employed by Ezra Stuart. Recent incidents, though minor in nature, were responsible for a growing tension between the two ranches. When discussing the situation with his daughter he had always underplayed their importance, insisting that the difficulties with the High Hill riders were nothing more than a series of misunderstandings that would soon be forgotten – but when he lifted down his Winchester from the pegs above the door, Cassie couldn't hide her surprise and concern.

'Dad!'

'Thought perhaps I'd see a pronghorn,' he explained. 'Get some fresh venison for the pot.' He offered a smile before turning on his heel and leaving the house.

Alarmed by flimflam that was so foreign to his nature, Cassie followed her father outside, hoping for an additional comment, reassurance that all was well. However, he spoke only to Butte, ordering the dog to remain on the porch while he strode across the yard. Cassie could see that his horse was already saddled and tied to the fence close to the place where Charlie Ute waited in motionless silence. Butte stood at her side, in eager anticipation of a reprieve from the order he'd been given, his ears pricked for the command to follow. When it didn't come, he sat under the window to await their return. With a brow creased with concern, Cassie returned to the house and closed the door.

Few words were spoken as Brad Edmond and Charlie Ute covered the five miles to the elbow of the river at an easy lope. Staying away from the recognized trail, they cut across the grassland and sat atop a bluff watching the men below without betraying their presence. Charlie's information had been accurate. The men below were from Ezra Stuart's High Hill spread. The top hand, Rex Coulter, was mounted, one leg cocked around the high roping horn while he observed and spoke to the four other men who were busy in the river.

'What are they doing?' Brad muttered, more to himself than in expectation of enlightenment from Charlie. In fact their behaviour barely needed explanation, as their activities were consistent with men panning for gold. It was the incongruity of the spectacle that puzzled Brad. The men were High Hill cattle-pushers, not prospectors. Even so, they had no reason to be here. Although this was a rugged corner unsuitable for the plough, it was still his land through which the stream was running. 'Wait here,' he told Charlie, guessing that the old Ute would be reluctant to become more involved.

Keeping to a gulley that obscured his descent, Brad reached the riverside downstream of the place where the men were working. Less than twenty yards separated them when he emerged on to the bankside trail. The men in the water had their backs to him and only stopped their chatter when, by replacing his right foot in the stirrup and turning his mount to face the approaching rider, Rex Coulter drew their attention to Brad's arrival.

The unsheathed rifle that lay across Brad Edmond's lap added to the tetchiness apparent in his tone when he spoke. 'What are you men doing here?'

Rex Coulter wasn't the sort of man easily cowed, and showing contrition for trespassing was the last thing he intended doing. Riling Brad Edmond had always been his intention. The manner in which his lips stretched in a grin was nearer a smirk than a sign of friendliness. 'Just stopped to cool our feet,' he said. His words earned rough laughter from someone in the river.

Brad let his eyes roam over the men in the water, making it clear that he was aware of the utensils they were using. 'You've got no business here,' he said. 'This is my land. Mount up and ride on.'

'That's not very neighbourly, Mr Edmond. Men just want water for themselves and their animals.'

'You've been here long enough to have had your fill. Git, and in future stay on your own range.'

Rex Coulter laughed, unpleasantly. 'This will be High Hill land when Mr Stuart takes it.'

Brad Edmond stiffened at the other's words. Despite the recent run-ins with his ranch hands, Brad had always had an amicable relationship with his more powerful neighbour. Never before had Ezra Stuart intimated that he wanted his land. 'I don't know what plans Mr Stuart has, but you can tell him to leave this spread out of them. I'm not moving from here.'

'That might not be a wise trail to follow. When Mr Stuart wants something, he gets it. One way or another.'

'He's not getting my land,' declared Brad. 'I'm hanging on to it and everything it holds.' His final words were accompanied by a gesture towards the men in the river.

Again, Rex Coulter offered a sly grin. 'Do you think you're capable of keeping a gold strike to yourself?' he asked. 'When word gets out you'll have a hundred men panning along this stretch inside a week.'

'If there's gold in that river it belongs to me. The law will be on my side, and you, Mr Coulter, and every prospector in the country will have to seek elsewhere along the river. Now, get on your horses and clear off.' Brad raised his rifle to back up his words.

'We'll go,' said Rex Coulter, 'but we'll be back.' He waited until the other men had packed away their pans and tools and climbed into their saddles. With a final, almost disparaging look at Brad Edmond he spoke again, reminding him of the earlier boast on behalf of his boss. 'One way or another,' he said, then led his men away along the riverside road.

Brad watched them until they were gone from sight before riding slowly away in the opposite direction. Assuming that Charlie Ute was watching from some place in the high ground he raised an arm and pointed ahead. It was an invitation to rejoin him further along the trail.

As soon as they were hidden from sight among the trees, Rex Coulter reined his horse to a halt. The other men followed suit and all sat silently for a moment until they were assured that they weren't being trailed by Brad Edmond.

It was Pol Glendale who spoke first, his voice as deep as a growling grizzly, which was apt for a man of his build and ginger colouring. 'What was all that talk about the boss?' he asked Rex Coulter. 'You said that we're the only people who know about the gold.'

'We are,' Rex assured him, 'but Edmond will be more troubled if he believes the whole of High Hill is against him.'

'We should have finished him,' Pol Glendale declared.

'If you recall, he had us at a disadvantage,' Rex Coulter reminded him. 'His finger was permanently on the trigger. He would have shot anyone who went for their gun.'

'It needs to be done if we want that gold,' Pol argued. 'Now that he knows what we're after he'll be on constant guard and try to keep it all for himself.'

Larry Grimes spoke up. 'Are we sure there's gold in that river? We haven't found a speck between us. Perhaps that old prospector was just stringing you along, Rex, bumming drinks on the strength of dreams in his head.'

'Do you take me for a fool?' Rex Coulter said. 'He showed me some nuggets, I tell you. There's gold all right, perhaps we just need to work another section.'

Pol Glendale butted in. 'We've got to do something about Edmond,' he declared, 'and we need to do it now before he spreads the news or informs the Elkhill sheriff.'

'What do you mean?' asked Larry Grimes, 'Kill him?'

'That's the best way to keep him quiet. We can work the river unhindered before the land falls into the hands of a new owner. That'll take months, by which time we'll have made our fortunes and be gone from this territory.'

'Pol's right,' said Rex Coulter. 'There'll be no witnesses out in this empty stretch of land. It'll be easy enough to put the blame on rustlers.'

'Come on, then,' said Glendale, 'what are we waiting for?'

'Perhaps it's a one man job,' Rex proposed. 'He's more likely to make a run for it if he hears a gang on his trail.'

Pol Glendale barely paused. 'I'll do it,' he said, slapping the stock of the weapon under his right leg. 'He'll never know what hit him.'

Brad Edmond hadn't travelled far from the place where he'd confronted the High Hill riders. In his mind he was trying to make sense of Rex Coulter's words. How did Ezra Stuart know there was gold in the river, and if it could be found in the stretch that ran through his land then surely it could also be found as it wound through the hills of no man's land? Why was it necessary to threaten to take his land when the wealth could just as easily be extracted elsewhere? But he wasn't an expert on mineral matters, nor, he suspected, was Ezra Stuart. In the morning, he resolved, he would ride out to the High Hill spread and confront Ezra. If talking didn't provide a solution he would ride into Elkhill and seek advice from Sheriff Hayes.

When he heard the horseman behind he didn't look over his shoulder. His first thought was that Charlie Ute had ridden down from the hillside, but then the pace with which the rider was approaching cast doubt in his mind. Before he got the chance to turn he was struck forcibly in the back and was flung forwards. For a moment, he clung on to his animal's neck before falling from the saddle to the hard ground below. The roar of the shotgun still reverberated as he hit the ground. Unable to move, barely able to breathe, he looked up at the sky. A moment later a mounted figure loomed over him. Pol Glendale didn't speak, merely looked down dispassionately, then raised the shotgun to his shoulder and slipped his finger inside the trigger guard.

TWO

After crossing the river, Walt Ridgeway paused. The exact location of Elkhill was unknown to him. Water, he knew, was essential for settlements to flourish, so following the river seemed the logical route. However, the riverside trail was heading upstream, west towards the Rockies and the little information he'd gathered told him that the small Montana township was still some miles to the north. The trail away from the river seemed to skirt some high ground and beyond that, Walt expected, would be the rich grassland for which the territory was famous and which supported the vast cattle herds of the northern ranches.

Barely had he opted for the route through the high ground than he reined his mount to a halt again. A solution to his dilemma seemed to be at hand. From up-river, a lone rider came into sight, emerging from around a distant outcrop that marked a bend in the trail. He rode in unhurried fashion, like a man who had travelled this stretch of

15

territory many times before. From time to time he raised his eyes to the high ground, casually searching the surrounding country. So when a second man came into view, riding hard and closing quickly on the man ahead, Walt assumed they were companions. The discharge of the shotgun, the back-shooting, took him by surprise, and it wasn't until the man pointed the gun at his un-horsed quarry that Walt found his voice and yelled.

Startled by the shout, and aware that his unprovoked attack had been witnessed, Pol Glendale lifted his eyes from the man on the ground. More than fifty yards separated him from the stranger astride the bay saddle-horse. A saddle-tramp, Pol guessed, a drifter looking for work, a man of no account. Pol raised his shotgun and fired the second barrel in the direction of the newcomer. The cartridge exploded, spreading the pellets almost wastefully into the space between the mounted men. The couple that stayed on course long enough to clip Walt's shoulder did so without sufficient force to cause any real damage.

Walt wasn't sure at what stage he'd pulled his Winchester from its scabbard, it had been an instinctive reaction, but by the time Pol had pulled the trigger his surprise had been overcome and he was governed by a need for self-preservation. He returned fire, the distance between them too small to diminish his accuracy or the weapon's power.

The .44 bullet smashed into Glendale's body, twisting him in the saddle and forcing a shriek of pain from his mouth. The shotgun fell from his grasp as he struggled to stay aboard his horse. Somehow he turned it and directed it back along the trail, swaying in the saddle as it gathered speed. It seemed that he was bound to fall, but horse and rider were still united when they reached the outcrop that marked the bend in the trail. When they disappeared from sight, Walt spurred his own horse forwards to tend to the shot man.

Brad Edmond was still alive, but barely so. His eyes were open and his lips moved, but no words were discernable. Death's pallor lay upon his skin, and his cheeks sagged like uncooked dough, but he raised a hand to grip Walt's sleeve. He was trying to communicate, but the knowledge that death was close was evident in his futile attempts to be understood.

Walt spoke gently, but was unsure what assistance he could give the stricken man. He hadn't any medical skills capable of easing his suffering – he doubted if anyone had – but it seemed un-Christian to let him die on the dusty road. Perhaps the man's home was nearby, but Walt had no knowledge of the area, didn't know how close he was to any ranch house or place of shelter. Besides, trying to move the man could be fatal for him. Walt was resigning himself to sitting with him until he expired when a slight movement alerted him to the fact that he was not alone. He turned swiftly, reaching for his sidearm as he did so, wary that the man he had shot had returned to wreak revenge.

The scrawny figure of morose Charlie Ute mounted on a droop-headed paint lifted from Walt's mind any concern he'd had for his own safety. 'Do you know this man?' he asked.

Charlie answered with a slow head movement.

'Did you see what happened?'

Another nodded response.

'Where does he live?'

Charlie extended his left hand, pointing the way through the high ground that Walt had recently deduced would be his best route to Elkhill.

Between them, they got Brad Edmond on to Walt's horse, and with Walt sitting behind to prevent him falling, they headed for his home. They travelled slowly, Charlie Ute acting as guide and leading Brad's horse. It took almost an hour to reach the small ranch house. Darkness had descended. A lamp had been lit and hung on a nail beside the door. Butte, who'd long been waiting on the porch to welcome home his master, stood silently when the men rode up to the yard gate.

The sound of horses informed Cassie that her father was not alone. This time, she thought, setting a place for Charlie Ute at the table had not been in vain. Doubtless the lateness of the hour would signify that the men were returning with mighty appetites. She was lifting the lid from the stew pot when the door was thrust open in startling fashion. Her immediate alarm at the sight of three men trying to gain simultaneous entrance quickly changed to anxiety. It was clear that it was only due to the effort of his companions that the man in the middle was able to cross the threshold. Each had one of his arms draped around their neck, and only by partly carrying and partly dragging him were they able to bring him indoors.

Cassie recognized the stricken man as her father, but was unsure if he was alive or dead. His eyes were closed and his features were altered by unconsciousness. The facial muscles were no longer tensile, and the covering skin was slack and without colour. 'What's happened?' she wanted to know.

'He's been shot,' one man told her. It barely registered with her that this man was a complete stranger.

Opening a door that led into a room at the rear of the building, Cassie pointed to a bed on which her father could be lain. Only when they put him face down did she see the remnants of the bloodied, tattered shirt that clung to her father's back.

'Who did it, Charlie?' she asked.

Walt Ridgeway deemed that there were more important matters to attend to. The man had lost a lot of blood, probably too much, but if he was to have any chance of survival some effort to stem the flow and proper treatment of the wounds was necessary. 'You need to get a doctor here quickly.'

'There's only Doctor Cairns in Elkhill.' Cassie spoke almost reflectively, as though unsure how to proceed. She looked into Walt's face for the first time, and ignoring the fact that she had never seen him before, asked him to ride and seek out the medic and bring him back to the ranch.

'I don't know the route to Elkhill,' he announced. 'In the dark I could miss the town, ride miles in the wrong direction. Your father needs the attention of a doctor as soon as possible.'

'Charlie?' Cassie turned her attention to the Ute. She knew he avoided the town, but the stranger's calm assessment of the situation had invoked her own urgency for assistance. She would do whatever she was capable of doing to clean the wounds and staunch the bleeding, but she doubted her ability to save her father's life without expert assistance.

In his usual taciturn manner, Charlie Ute accepted the task, quitting the ranch house with little more than a nod of farewell. Within moments, the sound of his horse's racing hoofbeats had died away.

Bathing the blood from her father's back proved difficult for Cassie. The shredded material of his old work shirt had been blasted into the open wounds. Even though he was senseless, from time-to-time her father flinched and murmured as though her ministrations were causing him greater pain. When she was done, she accepted Walt Ridgeway's advice and assistance, and piled flour into the lacerations and bound them tightly. When she'd finished, her father opened his eyes. She gripped his hand and spoke words of comfort to him.

Walt Ridgeway left them alone and stepped into the night. When he opened the door, the dog, Butte, stood motionless, watching, waiting for a word of instruction as though aware that there would be no more commands from his old master. Walt figured it could smell the other man's blood on him, legitimizing him as his replacement. Near the barn he could make out a long, low trough where he could clean his hands, but first he led the horses to it. Butte tagged along at his heels. He allowed the animals to drink long, then, trespassing on hospitality, led them into the barn. After unsaddling them, he tethered them and forked hay into their separate stalls. When he went to use the pump at the trough, the dog remained in the barn, settling itself near the stalls as though there were things to discuss with his equine friends.

Walt scrubbed himself with the cold water before returning to the house.

THREE

Rex Coulter suppressed a grin when the reverbera-
tions of the sound caused by the first distant shotgun
blast reached the ears of the slow-riding group, but
he couldn't hold it back when the second followed
shortly after. Glances were exchanged among the
men, all well aware of the meaning of those shots –
though not everyone was in accord with the deed
they indicated. Like the others who had been let into
the secret by the top hand, Larry Grimes had been
keen enough to fill his pockets with gold. He'd even
compromised his own principles for it, had been persuaded to pan the river on another man's property
because he'd been assured that such a lode could not
be found elsewhere within a hundred miles. It was
stealing, but if Brad Edmond didn't know it was
there, he wouldn't miss it when it was gone. But
murder, that was another matter altogether. They
would all swing for the cold-blooded killing of the
rancher.

That thought was still passing through Larry's

mind when the echo of a third shot, sharper, the crack of a rifle, reached the men. The unexpected sound of a second gun had an immediate effect on the High Hill riders. As one, they brought their horses to a halt, all eyes turning to Rex Coulter, seeking some kind of explanation, some reassurance that Pol Glendale's crime hadn't been thwarted, thereby putting their own future in jeopardy.

Demanding silence so they would pick up the sound of any pursuit as soon as possible, Rex Coulter looked back along the trail. More than two minutes passed before they heard the thundering hoofbeats of a fast running horse. Rex ordered everyone off the trail, to seek refuge among the bushes and trees that lined the trail. It was Chuck Morrison who first recognized the dun-coloured cow pony when it came into sight.

'It's Pol,' he said.

The relief that his companions felt at those words was soon replaced by shouts of concern. It was clear that all was not well with Pol Glendale. He was slumped forwards, barely clinging on, his head alongside his mount's neck, almost reminiscent of a raiding Cheyenne warrior. The horse was galloping wide-eyed, uncontrolled.

'Catch it,' yelled Rex Coulter.

Chuck Morrison was the first to react, intercepting the animal as it passed, grasping the bridle and riding alongside until it ceased its flight. In an effort to free itself from Chuck's restraint, it threw its head high, but succeeded only in dislodging Pol from the saddle. The shot man hit the hard ground and lay still. Blood seeping from his chest wound was making a fast growing stain on his shirt. Soon, all the men had dismounted to gather round the stricken man.

Rex Coulter showed little concern for Pol Glendale's injury. 'Did you get old man Edmond?' he wanted to know. 'Did he shoot you?'

Dredging up answers was painful. Pol's face twisted with the agony of effort, the short breaths he was capable of taking causing convulsions and his words like wisps of wind, too light to ruffle the hairs on a gooseberry.

Chuck Morrison, kneeling beside Pol, repeated the question. 'Who shot you?' It was necessary to put an ear to Pol's lips to catch his answer. Chuck looked up to relay the information. 'A stranger shot him. Someone waiting along the trail for Brad Edmond.'

'A witness,' muttered Larry Grimes.

'Shut up,' Rex snapped, then turning his attention back to Pol Glendale, repeated his first question. 'Is Edmond still alive?'

There was no response. Never would be. Pol's eyes were open wide but seeing nothing, and his mouth was agape, but neither words nor air would pass through it again.

'What do we do now?' Larry Grimes wanted to know.

Rex Coulter was sizing up the situation in his mind. Eventually he spoke. 'Chuck, ride back along the trail. Find out if Brad Edmond is still alive. If he isn't, we've got nothing to worry about. If the man who shot Pol is a stranger to the territory then he has no way of connecting the killing to the High Hill ranch.'

'And if Pol didn't succeed?' asked a nervous Larry Grimes.

'We'll finish the job for him. Now, load Pol on to his horse and let's get back to the ranch.'

They were yet a mile from the ranch when Chuck Morrison brought the news that, although wounded, Brad Edmond was still alive. 'I spotted them before they got clear of the high ground,' he reported. 'They were travelling slowly, old man Edmond was being held in the saddle. He looked bad. Perhaps he won't survive.'

Rex Coulter's concern was that Brad Edmond had already given details of his shooting to his rescuers. 'Who was with him? he wanted to know.

'One was a stranger but the other was that old Indian, Charlie Ute.'

No sooner had Chuck spilled his news to the others than another rider hove into view. He was heavily built but he sat easily on his mount like a man who had spent much time in the saddle. He wore a brown cord jacket and a smart white hat, which instantly identified the owner of the High Hill ranch to his employees. His gaze had instantly fallen on the bundle slung across one of the horses.

'Who's that?' he asked, his voice sharp, accustomed to obedience and instantaneous responses to his questions.

'We've got trouble, Mr Stuart,' Rex Coulter announced.

The other men remained silent, content to let the top hand do the talking, but they were to be surprised by the story he told.

'What do you mean? What's happened?' asked Ezra Stuart.

Rex's original plan had been to hide Pol Glendale's body and deny any involvement in the shooting of Brad Edmond. However, the news that that man was still alive called for other tactics. Silencing him for good had to be done quickly, and a scheme to achieve that with the help of his boss had begun to take shape in his head.

'Brad Edmond's brought in a hired gun. He's killed Pol Glendale.'

'A hired gun!'

'Edmond has been argumentative and making threats against High Hill for some time now. I told you he means to ruin you, Mr Stuart.'

Ezra Stuart's brow crinkled with lines of concern. His top hand had spoken of recent angry confrontations with his neighbour, but there had been no intimation that it would lead to violence. 'I don't understand it. I've known Brad Edmond a long time. We've never had disputes in the past.'

'We were crossing the river down by the bluff. We've always crossed his land at that point but today he stopped us, warned us off his land.'

'Why?'

'He means to divert the river. Cut off the loop that brings it on to our bottom range.'

'He can't do that.'

'Seemed like he was marking out a route from the bluff towards the Big Lake. Excavating a four-mile channel would be a costly undertaking for him but it would mean ruin for you, Mr Stuart.'

Ezra Stuart frowned. There hadn't been land disputes in the territory for several years but the memories of range wars were never buried. If another one threatened he knew that decisive action would be necessary.

'When Pol voiced an objection he was shot dead. Tell your boss that the same thing will happen to anyone else who tries to stop me, he said.'

'He won't get away with this. One of you boys ride into Elkhill and tell the sheriff I want to see him.'

'Boss, if he wants a war, you won't find anyone here reluctant to fight for you. Pol was our friend and we don't mean to let his killer get away with it.'

Ezra Stuart looked around the group, then at the body slung over the horse.

Rex Coulter spoke again. 'Boss, I reckon Edmond has been planning this for some time. Could be he's already spread some story about to provide himself with an alibi. The law's a joke when it comes to meting out justice. We can ride over to Edmond's place tonight. Him and his guns won't be expecting an attack. We can put a stop to the scheme before it goes any further.'

Thoughts flashed through the ranch owner's mind, memories of the lawless days when he'd solved his own problems and fought to hang on to what he owned. Now the sheriff was supposed to settle all disputes. Well, he had as much respect for the rule of law as any of his neighbours but he wasn't going to watch his cattle die of thirst while lawyers argued over the rights and wrongs of the matter.

'You're the one he means to ruin,' said Rex, driving in the final nail.

The men were gathered in the bunkhouse after the evening meal. Weapons were being checked and spare ammunition was being pushed into belt loops and pockets. Few words were being spoken but an uneasy atmosphere pervaded the long wooden building. It was Larry Grimes who, when he spoke to Rex Coulter, gave voice to his concern, wanted an explanation for the story that had been concocted.

'If Brad Edmond dies and the truth comes out, we'll all hang,' Rex Coulter told him. 'We don't want that, do we? So we've got to finish him off before he tells his version.'

Larry was still concerned: 'But there are people who already know. Charlie Ute and the stranger.'

'Perhaps they know that Pol shot Edmond, but there's no reason to suppose that they knew we were involved. We've got to keep it that way.'

'What if they saw him talking to us at the river and tell the sheriff?'

'Then he'll come here to ask his questions and we'll deny any involvement and then there's nothing the sheriff can do about it. Even if he listens to Charlie Ute, the sheriff isn't going to charge us on the strength of anything he says. No jury will convict on the word of an Indian.'

'And the stranger?'

'If he's just some saddle bum passing through the territory he won't be able to identify us. He's probably half-way to Lame Deer by now.'

'I don't like it,' said Larry Grimes. 'You shouldn't have sent Pol after him.'

'You'll like the gold well enough, won't you? Sometimes it's necessary to take drastic action to get what you want. Now,' he addressed everyone in the room, 'let's saddle up. The boss will be waiting for us.'

FOUR

With little commotion, Walt Ridgeway slipped inside the dimly lit house. The place was shrouded with an uncomfortable stillness, reminding him that he was an interloper at a very private family occasion. His eyes roved to the open doorway leading into the bedroom. He paused before crossing to it, unsure if his presence would be of benefit to the young woman, or construed by her as an unwanted intrusion – but the matter was decided for him when a sound reached him from within. The noise, a cross between a sob and a grunt, was being wrenched from the girl.

It took only a moment for Walt to take in the scene when he reached the doorway. The man was dead and his daughter was struggling to turn him over. Alive, the width of his shoulders and depth of his chest had been the measure of the strength he'd needed to build his home, plough his land and work his animals; in death they constituted a weight too great for his daughter to budge.

'Let me,' Walt said as he stepped into the room.

'I don't want him face down,' Cassie said.

There was something wild, desperate about her appearance. Her eyes were red-rimmed but wide open and dry. They were fixed on Walt with the sort of intensity he'd seen in others shocked by sudden, violent death. For a moment he rued his decision to leave her alone with her father. The horses wouldn't have come to any harm if they'd remained tied to the rail until morning, but he'd hoped the man would hang on to life until the doctor arrived. It seemed he'd been closer to death than Walt had judged, and perhaps his end had been reached in agony, not an easy thing for anyone to witness.

'Perhaps we should let the doctor see him before we move him,' Walt advised. He was thinking that shotgun pellets extracted from the body would be compelling evidence of murder to a judge and jury.

'No.' Some thought in Cassie's mind troubled her. Her father, she insisted, should be on his back, looking up at the sky.

Walt explained why he wanted the doctor to examine him before he was turned but he wasn't sure she was grasping the meaning of his words. 'I won't leave until the doctor has finished,' he told her. 'We'll make sure that your father is properly prepared for burial.' He closed the dead man's eyes before pulling a sheet over his head, then, although objections lingered on her lips and her reluctance to leave him thus was evident by her faltering steps, Walt took her out of the room.

Although their acquaintance was slight, Walt experienced a wave of sympathy for the dead man's daughter. This was due primarily to the circumstances that had brought them together, but it was coupled with his usual role of taking command in any situation. The girl, she couldn't yet be twenty, was pale, but Walt quickly attributed that solely to her sudden grief. Her body was well formed, lithe and strengthened, he supposed, by constant work around the ranch yard, and despite being tear stained, her face denoted intelligence and resolve. Her fair hair was pulled back into a pony tail that was tied with a length of maroon ribbon. It was the only bit of colour in her attire, as her trousers were faded blue denim and her shirt was grey and unadorned with jewellery or bright buttons.

Walt wondered what would happen to her now, whether she had family or friends nearby. No doubt she would have to sell the ranch. If she now owned all the land he'd crossed from the river it would be too much to manage alone. A thought niggled in his mind that even when her father was alive it was a lot of territory to manage without help. Yet there had been no other men around the yard when he'd brought her father home, and it was Charlie Ute who'd gone to Elkhill in search of the doctor.

It was Cassie, however, who opened the conversation. As the initial impact of her father's death began to clear from her mind she became aware that she was alone with a man who was a complete stranger.

He'd done nothing to cause her alarm, indeed he'd been helpful, discreet and considerate, yet she was becoming more aware of his physique and strength. She knew she wasn't really afraid of him, but she couldn't ignore the fact that she knew nothing about him.

'Who are you?' she asked.

'My name's Walt Ridgeway,' he told her. 'I was making my way to Elkhill when your father was attacked.'

'Do you know who did it?'

'I only know one person in this neighbourhood, Miss, and it isn't the man who shot your father.'

'What did he look like?'

'I didn't get a close look.'

'Would you know him again if you saw him?'

'I can't be sure.'

'What happened?' Cassie asked. 'I don't under-stand why anyone would want to kill Pa.'

'There's not much I can tell you. I'd crossed the river and was trying to decide the best route to Elkhill when your father came into view. A few moments later he was followed by another man who fired his shotgun at your father's back. He would have fired the second barrel if I hadn't fired at him.'

'Did you hit him?' she asked anxiously, surprised by the news that this stranger had retaliated on behalf of her father, and, when Walt nodded, wanted to know if the attacker had been killed.

'I don't know,' he confessed. 'I didn't follow when

he rode away. Attending to your father was my priority.'

'Was he alone?'

'I didn't see anyone else until the Ute showed up
to guide me here.'

Ruminatively, Cassie muttered Charlie's name.
She remembered that it was his earlier visit that had
taken her father from home. 'Did he see anyone
else?' she asked.

'I don't know. He didn't say a word on the way
here.'

'No. Charlie doesn't talk much. Especially to
strangers.'

'Perhaps he'll open up when he returns with the
doctor. How soon can we expect them?'

Cassie shrugged. 'Depends how quickly he finds
the doctor, and if the doctor's prepared to risk the
journey at night. If he does, he'll use the riverside
trail which is easier for a buggy. Perhaps they'll be
here in two hours, perhaps it'll be morning.'

Hardly had the words been spoken than they were
alerted by a noise outdoors. From the distant stable
Butte's barking could be heard.

'They're here,' said Cassie, her words edged with
confusion, disbelief that Charlie Ute could have
been to Elkhill and back so quickly – and something
else troubled her, though the cause escaped her.
Still, as Walt Ridgeway crossed the room to open the
door she began to turn up the brightness of the table
lamp to welcome the doctor.

Perhaps the ungraspable thought troubling Cassie

was the same one voiced by Walt as he opened the door. 'I didn't hear any horses,' he said.

Standing in the doorway, holding the edge of the door with his right hand, he peered into the darkness beyond. There was no buggy in the yard or saddle horses tied to the rails, but figures moved near the fence, and there was more movement around the water trough. A gruff voice came out of the night. 'That must be the gunhawk,' and the first shot ripped a slice of wood out of the doorframe close to Walt's head.

Reacting instinctively, intent upon becoming a smaller target for the gunman, he dipped his shoulders and bent his knees. In his eagerness however, it had the effect of unbalancing him. He toppled backwards and fell into the house, as more shots were fired. Some struck the building and a couple screamed through the room, thudding against the rear wall.

The guns fell silent for a moment but the gruff voice yelled again. 'Get the killers!' Another volley of hot lead was discharged at the house.

Lying on the floor, Walt used his feet to kick the door closed. He could see a thick timber bar propped against the wall that could be slotted into brackets on the door and wall to form a barrier. His first instinct was to secure the door, but concern for Cassie prompted him to a throw a glance into the room.

Bullets whistling into her home had frozen her into immobility. She hadn't moved away from the table, and was illuminated by the now bright lamp.

'Get down,' Walt yelled, and forsaking his first intention, which was to barricade the door, he scrambled across the floor to reach her. He grabbed her arm and pulled her down alongside him just as a bullet shattered a window and an ornament on the dresser at the far side of the room exploded into a thousand fragments.

He shook her, tried to alert her to the danger, but eventually had to slap her sharply to remove the glazed stare from her eyes. Her lips quivered for a moment, but he made her look into his eyes and tried once more to find words that would give her strength.

He gave a command, 'Stay on the floor,' then scuttled back to the door to put the bar in place. Bullets struck the building, a minute-long salvo of hot lead that smashed the windows and peppered the walls. Walt could hear the *thunk* of lead against wood, but the timbers were too stout to be penetrated. Securing the door was just the first step to repelling the unexpected attack. The windows on each side of the door were the remaining weak points, and fastening their shutters became his next priority. He and Cassie would be easy prey for anyone who reached them from the other side.

Keeping low so that his head didn't show above the window's bottom ledge, Walt scurried to his right. The shutter took the form of small doors that met half-way across the window. Again, solid timber had been used in their construction, and Walt was confident that once closed they would provide adequate protection from the attackers' bullets. He flipped the right side closed, but as he reached for the other he heard a yell of warning from Cassie Edmond.

Walt Ridgeway didn't consider himself a quick-draw gunman but in that moment of necessity the Colt from his hip holster was in his hand and discharged at the window almost before the girl's shout had ended. From his low position, the bullet went through the window on a skyward trajectory. From the yell of surprise that came from the other side, Walt knew that he'd missed the man but had done enough to scare him away. He would think twice before coming close again. Like Walt's, the shot the man had fired had gone harmlessly up in the air. To deter another attempt by their assailant, Walt sent a second shot through the window, then hastily slammed the left-hand portion of the shutter into place and slotted home the retaining bar.

Acknowledging the part Cassie had played in his current survival with a nod in her direction, Walt then wasted no time in running to fortify the second window as he had the first. He knew that a well co-ordinated assault would have seen a simultaneous attack on all the weak points, but this hadn't happened. He was able to lock up this window unmolested. In military fashion, he pondered the possible reasons for the enemy's negligence. Perhaps the force consisted of only two or three men, or perhaps the leader had no tactical knowledge of mounting a siege. And perhaps they'd arrived over-confident of success. Butte's early warning had prevented them barging into the house unhindered, so every man had then followed his own instruction.

'Are there shutters on the windows in the rear rooms?' he asked when he was satisfied that they could stand off a further frontal attack.

Cassie nodded, but when she spoke her words reflected the confusion that showed on her face. 'Who are they? What do they want?'

Walt had no answers for her questions, he merely said, 'Let's barricade the other windows.'

Walt was more in the dark than the girl as to the cause of the attack, but the intention was clear: they meant to kill everyone within. So he had to proceed with caution, had to assume that gunmen were covering the door and windows and would let loose a volley at any movement they detected within. Adopting the same technique he'd used on the front windows, Walt crawled across the room in which the body of Brad Edmond lay and reached the window. Cautiously, raising his head until he could see over the bottom window ledge, he scanned the darkness beyond. Nothing moved, no lights shone, no sound carried to him. He closed and locked the shutters, then returned to the main room where he encountered Cassie.

'I've closed the shutters in my bedroom,' she said, her face showing more composure, dredging up reserves of determination and spirit that until this moment she hadn't known she possessed. 'Pa put them on the windows as protection against Sioux attacks. This is the first time they've been needed.'

'And you can't think of any reason for coming under attack like this?' Walt asked her.

She replied with a shake of her head.

Outside, someone was shouting, calling to the house. Walt put a reassuring hand on the girl's shoulder. 'Let's see what they want.'

It wasn't the bullet from Walt Ridgeway's Colt that caused Chuck Morrison to abandon his attack at the window; that had flown harmlessly into the night sky at a very steep angle. Instead, so close had he been when the gun was fired, that the accompanying flame had painfully seared his face and eyes. Pulling the trigger of his own weapon had happened involuntarily as he'd staggered backwards in temporary blindness. Even so, when the second shot from the house whistled close past his head his instinct for survival urged him to seek cover. Stumbling across the yard he'd collided with the corner of the water trough and amidst violent curses, fell gracelessly to the ground. Larry Grimes became his saviour, hauling him behind the trough and out of danger from any further shots from the house.

Rex Coulter, scowling at the stricken cowboy, wanted information. 'How many are in there?' he wanted to know. 'Did you see old man Edmond?'

'I didn't see anything,' grumbled Chuck Morrison. 'Can't see anything.'

'His face is burned,' Larry Grimes announced, the

tone reflecting his belief that this raid was a bad idea.

'Leave him alone,' Rex Coulter snapped back. 'He won't die. Start pouring lead at that house. Aim for the windows. Shoot anything that moves.'

Another of the men, Frankie Teal, called from across the compound. 'They've blocked up the windows. Our bullets aren't doing any damage.'

Rex Coulter had been top hand at High Hill for several years and, in Ezra Stuart's opinion, had proved worthy of the trust placed in him. Without a son to share the load and with more of his own time occupied with book work, the ranch owner had ceded many of the day-to-day functions to his foreman. No-one was surprised therefore when Rex took charge of the raid on the Edmond ranch and Ezra Stuart was content to suppress any niggling thought that he had acted too rashly by firing instantly at the hired gun without first seeking an explanation from Brad Edmond. Rex, he was sure, was working for the benefit of High Hill and the men were accustomed to taking their orders from him, more of which were currently being issued.

'Frankie, Tex,' Rex Coulter shouted, 'check the windows at the back. See if we can force an entry there.' As a mark of his frustration, he fired a couple of rounds at the house.

'That's wasting ammunition,' Ezra Stuart reprimanded.

'It's distraction. Keeping them occupied at the front while the boys sneak in through the back windows.'

Chuck Morrison moaned. Larry Grimes looked towards the ranch owner in the hope that Ezra Stuart would put an end to the siege. In the darkness, Larry's silent pleading went unobserved. Figures scuttled into view from the corner of the house.

'Those windows are boarded up, too.' Frankie Teal reported.

Rex Coulter cursed.

Ezra Stuart called out to the house, his voice strident as one accustomed to issuing orders. 'Brad Edmond. We need to talk.'

There was no response from the house.

'A good man was killed, Brad. A price has to be paid for that.'

Rex Coulter butted in, his voice coarser but carrying to those inside with no less clarity than that of his employer.

'You and your hired gun are gonna swing.'

From the house, Walt Ridgeway shouted in response. 'Are you the law?'

'Law enough,' replied Rex Coulter. 'We know how to shell out justice.' He fired his gun at the place where Walt's voice had sounded.

'Whoever you are, you've come to the wrong place. Brad Edmond is no longer here, and there never has been a hired gun in this house. There is, however, a young woman. What kind of men come storming the home of an innocent girl in such fashion?'

'That's right, Mr Stuart,' Larry Grimes said, 'Brad

41

Edmond has a daughter.'

'Be quiet,' Rex Coulter told him.

'Nobody's going to hurt the girl,' Ezra Stuart shouted.

'But we're not leaving,' Rex Coulter added, 'until the men responsible for killing Pol Glendale come out.'

'If Pol Glendale is the man who shot Mr Edmond in the back with a shotgun, then he deserved to die.'

'What's that?' Ezra Stuart wanted to know.

Rex Coulter spoke up. 'Ignore him, Mr Stuart. Just a hired killer trying to get his neck out of a noose by blackening the name of a good man.' He looked at the faces around him, sensed that he was losing their support. He needed to persuade Ezra Stuart to press on with the attack before they threw in their hands. 'We'll burn them out,' he said.

Larry Grimes recoiled at such a suggestion. 'We can't do that, Mr Stuart. The girl hasn't done anything to deserve that.'

Rex Coulter was dismissive of the younger man's concern. 'She won't be hurt. As soon as the smoke builds up they'll come out. We'll leave her alone.'

Larry Grimes no longer trusted Rex Coulter. In his opinion, the prospect of filling his pockets with gold had made the top hand much meaner.

Ezra Stuart hesitated. It would be difficult to justify their actions if young Cassie was killed.

'This is why we came, Mr Stuart. Edmond began this trouble by trying to ruin you. If he doesn't pay the price now he'll probably try again,' insisted Rex.

42

The ranch owner mulled over the situation, then slowly nodded his head.

'Get some kindling,' an elated Rex Coulter told the men around him.

Through the gun ports built into the shutters, Walt Ridgeway could see movement at the far side of the yard. Since the talking had ceased he figured they'd come up with another plan to get him out of the house. Cassie stood close to him, nervous but with her head held high, putting on a brave face.

'What will they do now?' she wanted to know.

'I'm not sure.'

'Why didn't you tell them that my father is dead?'

'I'm not sure about that, either,' he said, but in truth it was because he didn't believe it would make any difference. Perhaps they would have gone away satisfied with that knowledge, but he didn't think so. They hadn't come to talk or listen to explanations, they'd fired without warning, and if they meant to kill him without mercy it was probable that Cassie would suffer the same fate. He wasn't prepared to let that happen without a fight.

That was when he saw the first torch being lit and became instantly aware of their plan.

'Quickly,' he said, leading Cassie into the dark room where her dead father lay. 'We've got to get away from here.'

He hoped that all their attackers were congregated at the front of the house, and that no one was covering the rear windows. Cassie was confident that, once they were clear of the house, she could lead them to safety.

Keeping low, and moving it inch by inch, Walt opened the left half of the shutter. He paused a moment before starting on the other part. Then the window shattered and a bullet screamed over his head. Swiftly he closed the small wooden doors and barred them. There was no exit.

They went back to the front of the house and peered once again through the gun slit. Three men with burning brands were approaching the building at separate points.

Walt shouted a warning. 'I'll shoot if you come any closer!'

Rex Coulter replied. 'There's no way out for you.'

Walt knew there was little hope of survival for him. Perhaps he could shoot one or perhaps two, but once they got a flame to the building's timbers it would only be a matter of time until he was killed. He could feel a tremble run through Cassie, whose blue eyes had darkened with fear. Her lips were pressed together tightly to prevent any sound escaping. Although he didn't think it existed, he knew her only chance of survival was their mercy.

'Mr Edmond is dead,' he called, 'and his daughter can't hurt you. If she comes out, do you promise not to harm her?'

Everyone heard his words, and some of those in the yard thought that this would put an end to the siege. But not Rex Coulter. 'More lies!' he exclaimed. 'Throw those torches!' he shouted.

The three burning brands were launched through the air, each one reaching the porch which, unknown to those inside, had already been smeared with coal oil found in one of the outbuildings. The flames immediately took hold and the wood began to crackle.

Walt fired at the nearest arsonist, who emitted a yell of pain before stumbling away across the yard. The other two were running fast to get out of the glare of the firelight, which made them clear targets. They dived behind the water trough from where they could watch the rising flames and fire bullets at the building to emphasize the fact that there was no way out.

Walt fired a shot in their direction. It splashed in the water. He felt Cassie's hands gripping his shirt, then her face pressed against his back.

'We're not done yet,' he told her, though he didn't know what he could do to save them. He turned his attention once more to the yard, saw a movement near the gate and fired at it. The man threw up his hands as his knees buckled and he went down to the ground. As if it were a signal, one by one the attacking gang stopped shooting, and gathered around the shot man. Almost as suddenly as it had begun, the siege was over. When victory seemed to be within their grasp, the attackers collected their horses and departed the burning ranch. For Walt, it was reminiscent of Indian raids that petered out at the death of their leader, and he could now only wonder at the identity of the man he'd hit.

Who was the stricken man who had turned the tide in their favour?

FIVE

The first pink ribbons of dawn lit up the sky as Dr John Cairns drove his buggy through the gate into the Edmonds' ranch-yard. Charlie Ute, on his sleepy-looking cayuse, was ten yards adrift, hanging back as though doubtful of a welcome. When he reined to a halt just inside the boundary fence the buggy proceeded for another twenty yards in the direction of the house, stopping only when it came alongside the two figures who had watched their approach.

Their clothes, hands and faces smeared with soot and ash, their eyes red from smoke and their lips cracked and dried from the almost intolerable heat, Cassie Edmond and Walt Ridgeway had barely the energy to greet the medic and the Ute. At the end of the siege they had scrambled out of one of the rear windows to set about the task of defeating the blaze. For more than an hour they had battled side by side against the fire that threatened to devour the girl's home. The oil-soaked veranda was burning fiercely, and the small amounts of water that could be thrown

47

at it from filled buckets had no hope of quenching the flames. Instead, Walt had grabbed a shovel from the barn and thrown soil from the yard on to the timbers of the veranda. It was gruelling work, exacerbated by the heat of the growing inferno, like feeding a furnace without respite. He worked back and forth along the frontage, piling soil on to the floor of the veranda, burying the flames at their source. When the waist-high rails began to crackle and snap he used a long-handled axe to smash them down and scatter them across the open ground where they were left to burn away to ash.

Meanwhile, spurred by an instinct to cling on to her home and a fear that the body of her father would be consumed without the benefit of a preacher's words, Cassie, too, proved to be a prodigious worker. Ceaselessly she filled and carried buckets of water from the pump and threw them on the burning building. Because of the solidity of the timber with which it had been constructed, the front wall was burning less spectacularly than the veranda – but still the fire was eating its way slowly but inexorably through the wood.

When Walt had doused and smashed away the veranda, he assisted Cassie, she pumping water while he carried and threw the water at the burning walls. Despite their combined efforts it was likely that their work would have been in vain if nature hadn't come to their assistance. Rain, unexpected and heavy, fell from the skies, saturating the house until the building hissed and spluttered in the deluge and smoke was barely able to rise above the roof top.

Walt and Cassie opted to take shelter in the stable, their choice owing as much to a need to pacify the animals housed there as a need to get out of the rain. They had heard the horses stamping restlessly in fear throughout their fire-fighting endeavours, but had had no time to attend to them. In any case, despite the smells and noises that were reaching them, the horses were safe in the stable. They were only placated, however, when the pair slumped down in a pile of loose straw.

Cassie was spent, drained of her strength by the events of the night. Even though she was accustomed to helping out with the yard work, her arms and shoulders had never before ached in the way they did at that moment, and her trembling legs could not have held her upright a moment longer. Her exhaustion wasn't just physical, either: her ability to think had almost deserted her. The darkness that enveloped her when she closed her eyes seemed to be so deep as to be enticing her to a place where her pains and problems would be lost forever. The death of her father had changed her life forever. She was now alone in the world, without close friends or family to provide help or guidance in the days ahead.

Butte, who had remained in the stable and had been quiet since the shooting began, slunk forwards as though ashamed of his absence in her hour of need. He nudged with his brow but kept an eye on the stable door as he did so.

Opening her eyes, Cassie reached out and idly

rubbed his head in sympathy. 'He's looking for my father,' she told Walt. 'He doesn't like to be parted from him.'

It seemed, however, that this time Butte knew the parting was forever. Pining, he lay down and rested his head on Cassie's legs.

'He knows,' she said. 'How do they do that?'

Walt Ridgeway had no answer for the girl. At that instant, the instincts and communication methods of other animals held little interest for him. There were matters of greater importance to be considered, but he wasn't sure if this was the right moment to question the girl – or indeed, if he had the right to interfere in her business. But the men who had attacked the house had made it his business, had called him a gunhawk and tried to kill him, when the truth was that he'd stumbled accidentally into the situation. He'd only hung around to await the arrival of the doctor, but he couldn't help wondering what would have happened to Cassie if he hadn't remained with her. Such had been the determination of the attackers that Walt was certain they had not come to take prisoners. Yet strangely, they had abandoned their mission at the very moment that success seemed to be in their hands.

'Was there anything familiar about the voices that called to the house?' he asked, the question framed by his thoughts.

Cassie turned her head slowly in his direction. Her pale face was made spectral-like by the black shadows below her eyes, even her lips, small and dry despite the drenching she'd taken in the sudden downpour, showed little pinkness. Had there been something recognizable in the voices, she wondered – but the noise of gunfire and the fear it had instilled in her had driven away her ability to be sure of anything. She shook her head. 'No.'

'And you can't think of any reason for the attack?'

Cassie shook her head.

'Disputes with neighbours?'

Again she answered with a head shake – but was picturing her father lifting down his rifle from above the door. She hadn't believed his story of needing it to catch game, but had no other explanation for it. 'It was Charlie Ute who took Pa away from the ranch,' she said. 'Perhaps he can answer your questions.'

Shortly after, Cassie fell asleep, and Walt Ridgeway, too, dozed as he lay in the comfort of the soft straw. Butte's barking disturbed them. Wary that the gunmen had returned to finish off the job they'd begun, Walt drew his Colt before cautiously opening the barn door. The rain had ceased, and in the weak light of early morning he could make out the movement and shape of a buggy and two-horse team. Following the vehicle across the flat land beyond the boundary fence was a single rider on a low-running horse.

'It's Doctor Cairns.' Cassie had joined him, quietly, viewing the approaching company from behind Walt Ridgeway as though in need of his protection, but then stepping forwards briskly into the yard to be on hand to greet them.

'What's happened here?' John Cairns asked, stepping out of the buggy with his medical bag in his grasp.

'Some men came to make sure Cassie's father was dead,' Walt told him.

The doctor took in the scene of scattered embers, fire-scarred walls and broken window panes. 'Where is your father?' he asked Cassie.

'In the house, but you're too late. He died several hours ago.'

'I was making a call at the other side of town,' he said, adding 'I couldn't get here any quicker,' as though he thought they suspected he'd ignored the summons because it had been delivered by Charlie Ute. He picked his way across the soil-strewn veranda to the door. 'I'll take a look at him while I'm here.'

Walt stayed outside. If the doctor needed assistance he would call for it, but he figured Cassie would consider the examination of her father's body to be a private matter. Besides, he wanted to talk to Charlie Ute who had dismounted and was squatting against the paint's front legs, under its head, effectively preventing it from moving forwards. When Walt reached him he seemed to be observing the thin smoke streams that were still rising from the building, as though they contained a message that would be revealed by deep study.

'Do you know who did this?' asked Walt.

The scrawny Ute hadn't spoken when they had travelled together from the river, and it seemed that he wasn't yet prepared to break his silence. Charlie's distrust of white people was difficult to overcome. Still, Walt had to persist if he was going to get any information out of him.

'Mr Edmond was down by the river because you took him there. What did you show him?'

There was a moment when Walt suspected the older man wouldn't divulge anything, regarded him as a stranger who hadn't yet earned the necessary respect. Then suddenly, Charlie Ute held up his right hand, spreading the fingers then counting them off with the other index finger.

'Five,' said Walt. 'There were five men?'

Charlie nodded.

'Who were they, do you know?'

Charlie still didn't speak. Instead, he used a finger to draw in the dust. He marked out three vertical lines, the middle one longer than the outer two. The left-hand line began at the same top point as the longer centre line, while the right-hand ended equal with its bottom point. He connected the lines with horizontal bars, the left set higher than the right.

'What's that, Charlie? Is it a brand?' The expression on the Ute's face remained unreadable, but Walt took that to mean that he wasn't wide of the mark. 'They were from a neighbouring ranch?'

A troubling thought entered Walt's mind as he uttered the words, and when Charlie stretched out an arm and pointed north-east, that thought developed into a deeper concern. That was the direction in which he'd been heading before he'd become embroiled in the current affair. He looked again at the figure drawn in the dust. Did it represent conjoined Hs? 'High Hill?' he asked.

The resulting nod of assent gave Walt a cause for uneasiness which he did his best to hide.

'Why did they attack Mr Edmond? Did you see what they were doing?'

When Charlie spoke, Walt was taken by surprise. 'In river,' he said, and shuffled his hands in imitation of sieving water through a griddle. 'Seeking gold,' he explained.

At that moment, Cassie and the doctor emerged from the house and crossed the yard to join them.

John Cairns spoke to Walt Ridgeway. 'Cassie tells me that you witnessed the shooting of her father.'

'I'd just crossed the river down by Eagle Pass.'

'Judging by the number of pellets in Brad's body the shooter must have been very close when he fired.'

'It was a deliberate act to take Mr Edmond's life,' Walt told him. 'The killer would have used the other barrel on him if I hadn't interfered.'

'You shot the man?'

'I did. Perhaps there's another patient waiting for you when you get back to Elkhill.'

'You should report what you saw to the sheriff. He'll need your testimony in the event of a trial.'

'Charlie was a witness, too. He knows more about

54

this business than I do.'

'Oh.' The doctor's utterance held no encouragement for Charlie to relate what he knew. 'I suppose you, too, should tell the sheriff what you know,' he told the Ute, but the flat tone of his words made it clear that he didn't expect his story would ever be heard in a court of law.

'According to Charlie, the men were from the High Hill spread,' Walt said.

Doctor Cairns spoke to Cassie. 'I hadn't heard of any trouble between your father and Ezra Stuart.' At the mention of this name, the uneasiness aroused earlier by the possible involvement of High Hill now became more troubling, but the concern that registered momentarily on his face escaped the notice of Cassie and Doctor Cairns.

'I didn't know of any, either,' Cassie answered, but couldn't forget the manner in which her father had lifted down his rifle from its pegs above the door. Something, it seemed, had troubled him, but he hadn't confided in her.

'Perhaps you should come to town with me?' the doctor said. 'We can arrange the burial of your father in the town's cemetery.'

Cassie wouldn't contemplate such a plan. 'My father will be buried on his own land,' she insisted. 'Cy Cuttle and the boys will help me.'

'You've got a crew?' asked Walt. As Cassie had been alone when he'd brought her father home he'd assumed that they had neither the stock nor acreage to need assistance in running the place.

'They're with the herd on the bottom land,' she said. 'I need to get a message to them. Get them back here quickly.'

SIX

Despite his concern that the attackers might return, and also his need to complete his own journey, Walt Ridgeway accepted the task of seeking out Cassie Edmond's crew. But a feeling that he was deserting her in an hour of need nagged at him. In the main, however, it was Cassie's own brave stance that persuaded him that there was little more he could do at the homestead. Although the trials of the siege were, from time to time, still apparent by glints in her eyes and movements around her mouth, there was a stoic resolve that prevented her from allowing them to develop into signs of weakness: no tears, no trembling lips. She would not go to Elkhill with John Cairns, she announced, adding that this was her home and there was much work to be done. It was a display of the spirit he'd seen in other pioneer families, the attitude necessary for survival in isolated areas. No harm would befall her, she insisted, before her drovers returned, even repeating Walt's own voiced opinion that the cowardly behaviour to which they'd been subjected in darkness would not be repeated in daylight.

The doctor's affirmation that he would inform the sheriff of the events that had occurred further eased Walt's mind, and an unspoken promise gleaned from Charlie Ute's expression, assured him that that scrawny older man would remain near the house until protection for her arrived.

So he'd ridden away, an invitation to visit again whenever he was in the vicinity warm in his ears, and he'd followed the landmarks specified by Cassie until, from rising ground, he'd espied the small line cabin two miles ahead.

Undressed logs had been used in its construction. It had a low roof that sloped from front to back. Turf had been piled atop for insulation and a tin pipe from the stove below prodded another eighteen inches into the sky. The shack had been built half-way up a hill. Big pines stood tall behind, acting as some sort of protection when the worst weather of winter swept down from the north. But now it was summer and in the balmy warmth of mid-day, the view from the doorway was an unspoilt carpet of lush grassland.

To Walt's chagrin, the cabin was empty. He juggled in his mind the idea of awaiting the men's return, but soon discarded it. The men might not return from their work on the range until it was almost dark, and he was anxious to get someone back to the Edmonds' ranch house before nightfall. Nor did he want to be roaming unknown territory after sunset, either. He wanted to be in Elkhill as soon as possible. He rode up through the trees to the top of the hill which provided a panoramic view of the surrounding area.

Moving specks on the meadow that stretched from the high mounds to a ribbon of water soon caught his eye. It wasn't a large herd, perhaps three hundred head, grazing peacefully. A short distance from them, a thin, wispy smoke line climbed to the sky. Walt set his horse at a steady trot in that direction.

Two men close to the fire watched him warily as he approached. The elder, his face the colour of walnuts and almost as deeply creased, had adopted an open-legged stance that intimated authority. The legs of his coarse black trousers were hidden by leather chaps. A gun-belt was tied around his waist, above which an off-white heavy cotton shirt was worn below a brown waistcoat. The hat on his head had seen several winters but sat tightly on his brow, so Walt could see little of his greying hair.

The second man was younger. His black hat was pushed to the back of his head, his reddish-brown hair curling thickly as it jounced on his brow when he rose to his feet. 'Howdy,' he greeted.

'I'm looking for Cy Cuttle,' Walt explained. 'Got a message for him from the Edmond place.'

Walt wasn't surprised when the older man owned up to being Cuttle. He told him that his employer had been killed and that there'd been a further attack on the ranch house. 'His daughter needs help,' he added. 'You all need to get back quickly in case they try again.'

'Sure thing,' he said, then turning to the other man he said, 'Dave, fetch Lou. He can come back with me. You'll have to stay with the herd.'

'Is Miss Edmond OK?' Dave asked.

'She isn't hurt,' Walt replied. 'Best way to make sure she remains that way is to get back quickly.'

Dave acknowledged the advice with a nod, clambered into the saddle on his dun pony and rode away along the river to find the third man of the group.

For reasons of his own, Walt was eager to know the cause of the problem arising between Brad Edmond and Ezra Stuart, but Cy Cuttle was as much in the dark as everyone else.

'Can't say they've been acting on Mr Stuart's orders, but some of the High Hill riders seemed to be going out of their way recently to pick a fight with the boss.'

'What about?'

'That's just it, nothing specific. Just something or nothing. Making out he was acting high and mighty because he owned some land.'

'Was he?'

'Naw. Mr Edmond was too wrapped up in making his ranch a going concern to look down on anybody else. Only beginning to rebuild the herd after two bad winters.'

'And there were no other problems?'

'Not that I knew about. Apart from everyday ranch matters he didn't act as though he had any concerns.'

'What about his daughter,' Walt asked, 'does she have any family close by to give her advice?'

'Never heard talk of any. Far as I know her father came west after the war. Miss Cassie was born out here. There weren't any visitors even when her mother died.'

'She might turn to you for some guidance.'

'More likely she'll sell up and I'll be looking for work.'

Walt asked for the shortest route to Elkhill and climbed into the saddle before Dave had returned with the third man. 'By the way,' he said, before putting spurs to his horse's flanks, 'Charlie Ute did all he could to save Mr Edmond. You might acknowledge it by sharing coffee with him now and then.'

When they took Ezra Stuart's body back to High Hill, the story told to his daughter regarding his killing put the blame entirely on Brad Edmonds.

'He meant to ruin your family, Miss Connie,' Rex Coulter told the shocked young woman. 'He was planning to divert the water away from the bottom range and brought in a hired gun to back his play.'

Connie Stuart shed tears as she gazed on her dead father, his skull shattered by a single bullet. 'Brad Edmond will pay for this,' she vowed, the desire for vengeance twisting the usual attractiveness out of her face.

'Already has, Miss Connie. We left him dead and fired his home.'

'And the hired gun?'

'I imagine he perished in the flames.'

'Be sure that he did,' she snapped at the top hand. The harshness of her tone took Rex Coulter by surprise, but the demand that followed both excited and chilled him. Connie's words added to his confidence that he could escape all blame for the recent events. 'I want revenge on everyone connected with my father's death.'

'Do you want me to handle it?' he asked, knowing that his employer's blessing meant that he could use his authority in any way he deemed fitting.

'Yes.'

Rex held back the grin that sought to spread across his face. It wasn't just the uttered word of command to which he reacted, but the knowledge that at last she was showing a need for him that, in the past, had been rejected with disdain. To her he'd been no better than any other rider employed by her father, had barely noticed his existence or his efforts to earn her affection, but now, in this dark hour of need, it was to him she turned. Unexpected opportunities were now opened to him. Good fortune, he believed, had finally begun to favour him. Wealth would come with the fruition of the plans in place to take over the Edmond spread, and now, although he could never have Connie, he could control a major portion of influence wielded by High Hill. Connie was soon to marry, but she had chosen a husband who was not a cattleman. So handled correctly, the job of running the ranch would become his. By fulfilling her demand for revenge she would be forever in his debt, and High Hill's power could become his to wield.

The opportunity to appease Connie Stuart's appetite for revenge occurred later that day in Elkhill. Along with a couple of High Hill drovers, Rex rode into town with the purpose of imparting their version of the events that had culminated in the death of Ezra Stuart to Sheriff Hayes. The lawman, however, was out of town, leading a small posse south to investigate the ambush of the stagecoach from Bozeman. The driver had been wounded and the passengers robbed at gunpoint. The chance of catching the culprits was slim, but Hayes was not the kind of man to shirk his duty. The posse had been gone since early morning, and no one could say when they'd return.

Although they had managed to grab a few hours' sleep following their return to High Hill, Frankie Teal and Tex were still weary men when they reached Elkhill. Rex's exhortation to wait for him in Reno's Retreat, the saloon cruelly named because the ill-famed Major had brought his troops close to the site of the town as he made his way towards the Little Bighorn, was obeyed with alacrity. If Rex had other business to attend to first, that was the reason he was paid top dollar. They wouldn't drink all the saloon's beer before he rejoined them.

In fact, Rex's further business had nothing to do with High Hill. When he was sure that the two cowhands had lost interest in all things apart from the glasses in their hands, he darted down a back alley and made his way to the rear entrance of an office three blocks away. He tapped lightly against the door and waited. Sometimes he had to wait several minutes to gain admittance, but this day his knock was swiftly answered as the lawyer had no client in his office.

'Reckon you can go and make your offer for the Edmond place,' Rex Coulter told the elegant man who opened the door to him. 'Brad Edmond is dead.'

Jonathan Barclay examined his visitor's face for a sign that his words had been uttered as some kind of jest. 'Dead?'

'That's what you wanted, isn't it? Quick possession, you said, which ruled out trying to scare him off.'

'I suppose so.' The attorney reached for a bottle and a couple of glasses from a corner cupboard, his initial surprise replaced by an expression of contentment. He had merely been unprepared for the cow-hand's news, which represented a sudden, giant stride forwards towards the completion of his plan. Brad Edmond's death was unimportant. 'What happened? Can it be traced back to you?'

'I've got it covered,' bragged Rex. 'We're spreading the story that he was planning to drain the river loop that waters part of the High Hill range and that he brought in a hired gun to enforce it.' He related the events surrounding the death of Pol Glendale and the attack on the Edmond ranch.

'And you're sure Brad Edmond perished?'

'Reckon all inside perished in the fire,' he said,

'but I've been instructed by Miss Connie to ensure they did.'

'Connie ordered that?'

'Oh, didn't I tell you?' Rex Coulter grinned, unable to hide his belief that his next bit of news held special significance for himself, 'Mr Stuart was killed during the raid on the Edmond place.'

'Ezra Stuart, dead?'

'That's right. Miss Connie's now the boss of High Hill and I reckon she'll be depending upon me to run the ranch for her.'

'Her husband-to-be might have something to say about that.'

'He's a career soldier. What will he know about cattle?'

'Besides, there's the Edmond place. Our agreement is for you to take over there eventually.'

'Changed my mind,' said Rex. 'The power I'll yield as manager of the vast High Hill ranch will be greater than anything I could achieve as owner of the Edmond place. Instead of taking over what remains of that ranch when you sell off the mineral rights, I'll just take a bigger slice of the profit.'

'I see.' Jonathan Barclay's words were delivered without emphasis, but he was irked by the other's declaration. He'd become acquainted with Rex Coulter while conducting business on behalf of Ezra Stuart. Now, it seemed, Coulter was assuming the role of partner in the scheme, when he was nothing more than hired help. They'd agreed that the greater part of his payment would be in the form of

Brad Edmond's ranch, but that was because the lawyer had no interest in working cattle nor, indeed, the hard work that would be required to make it a viable business after it was stripped of its current stock and the land had been subjected to the demands of heavy mining traffic.

His real partner lived in Helena, a friend employed in the Territorial Offices. Fred Winterfield had come into possession of some interesting information. A geographical survey of the nearby hills had proved that there was no trace of gold, but rock samples had revealed enormous deposits of copper. According to Winterfield, the owner of the land around Eagle Pass would soon become very rich indeed. Brad Edmond hadn't been aware of his prize asset, but a public announcement would soon be issued, and Jonathan Barclay and his Helena-based friend had resolved to get their hands on the land as cheaply as possible before anyone at the Edmonds' ranch did. After selling the mineral rights to the highest-bidding mining company, they would divide the profit. That, however, would be a two-way split, and Rex Coulter wouldn't figure in it.

At that moment that very man gave a small shout of elation which grabbed the lawyer's attention. Rex Coulter was gazing out of the window, his eyes fixed on a figure in the shade of the overhang outside the sheriff's office. 'Look there!' he said. 'The last person capable of telling a different story. Lucky for us the sheriff is out of town. I reckon I'll have to fix that old Indian before Andy Hayes returns.'

Without another word, Rex Coulter quit Jonathan Barclay's office using the same door by which he'd gained admittance, and made his way to Reno's Retreat. He drew his two High Hill colleagues aside and spoke quietly.

'Charlie Ute's waiting outside the sheriff's office,' he told them. 'We can't let him talk to Andy Hayes. If he saw us working in the river everyone will know that there's gold to be found.'

'What can we do?' asked Frankie Teal.

'Miss Connie wants revenge on everyone involved in the death of her father. I reckon that includes Charlie Ute.'

Within moments Rex Coulter had gathered a crowd around him, proclaiming that Brad Edmond had hired killers to kill Ezra Stuart, perpetuating the lie that they were fighting over water. Brad Edmond was depicted as the aggressor and Ezra Stuart a peace-seeking victim. There were doubters in the room as to the validity of the story, but everyone agreed that the slaying of such a prominent figure was a shocking affair that would have repercussions throughout the area.

'Pol Glendale was killed, too,' shouted Rex Coulter, 'and Chuck Morrison is back at the ranch almost blinded by a shot that seared his face.' Sensing that he had most of the room in his thrall, he incited them further. 'One of those who assisted Edmond is out on the street at this moment,' he said. 'Charlie Ute was riding with Brad Edmond and his gunman when Pol was killed, and I guess he was one of the group who slew Mr Stuart when he went to talk to them.'

'Well, let's hold him until the sheriff gets back,' suggested someone.

'Let's string him up,' responded Rex Coulter. 'That's the way we deal with murderers, isn't it?'

There were one or two voices of dissent among the crowd, but there were many more, urged on by the shouts and gestures of the High Hill hands, who were prepared to take the law into their own hands. They followed Rex Coulter out of Reno's Retreat and waited while he grabbed the rope from his saddle.

'There he is,' he shouted, pointing at the bony figure leaning against the wall of the sheriff's office.

The crowd gathered pace as it advanced down the street. Cries of *murderer* and *string him up* drew the attention of other people on the street, and they joined the mob when the victim of the crime was revealed as Ezra Stuart.

Charlie Ute didn't like Elkhill, but he had promised Cassie Edmond that he would tell the sheriff that he'd been a witness to the shooting of her father. Confronted with a locked office, he'd hung around for a while, trying to be invisible to the townspeople but aware of the many looks of contempt that were thrown his way. Finally deciding that the sheriff's absence was not going to be of short duration, he'd been on the verge of leaving town when the angry bunch of men tumbled out of the saloon. Instinctively, even before the first voice was raised, he sensed that he was the target of the anger which imbued the group of men. Unfortunately he didn't react quickly enough. By the time the cries had tagged him with the title *murderer*, he was hemmed in by people who were gathering to listen to the shouts of the crowd.

'Don't let him get away,' Rex Coulter shouted and hands grabbed at Charlie, holding him while the crowd swarmed forward.

'Hang him,' someone shouted, and there was a commotion on the street as some people tried to get away from the area and others were anxious to get closer.

Charlie's arms were pulled behind his back and lashed together. He tried to struggle – he was strong in many ways – but force of numbers made escape impossible. They began to drag him along the street and Rex threw his loop over Charlie's neck as he was hustled towards the far end of town.

'What are you doing with that man?' demanded the stentorian voice of a portly man who rushed out of an office.

'He killed Ezra Stuart, Judge,' came the answer.

'Then it's a matter for the law. Take him to the sheriff.'

'He's out of town.'

'The man deserves a trial.'

'He's an Indian. That's guilt enough.'

Laughter greeted the comment, and didn't halt the march towards the stout oak tree in front of the newly erected church.

'Stop!' shouted the judge, but his protest was ignored, and Rex Coulter threw the loose end of his rope over an appropriate branch.

SEVEN

Someone had grabbed a keg from the long walkway in front of Basil Deepcut's store and stood it on end under the oak's flung-out bough, and Charlie Ute was roughly manhandled atop of it, gaunt with the knowledge that further resistance was hopeless. Escape was impossible, the mob was too great, their determination too intense.

The rope was taut around Charlie's neck when the horse around whose saddle the loose end had been tied was led forwards. Judge Hawkins shouted another vain protest against the proceedings, but was told in no uncertain terms that there would be no stay of execution.

'We'll save the town the cost of a trial, Judge,' Rex Coulter shouted. He pointed at the figure resigned to his fate, standing steadily on the small, up-turned barrel. 'He's guilty of murder. Get on with it,' he ordered.

Above the clamour a sudden gunshot cracked. A rider, his smoking pistol pointing skywards, used his

71

horse to nudge his way through the assembled lynch mob. Instantly, the hubbub dwindled to nothing, and people turned their attention to discover the identity of the new arrival. The only person who knew the intruder's identity was the man with the rope around his neck. The majority of townspeople, caught red-handed in an illegal act of violence by a stranger, shuffled aside guiltily and cleared a passageway through to the hanging tree for him.

'Release that man,' ordered Walt Ridgeway.

Rex Coulter, bullish, grabbed at the bridle around the head of Walt's horse. 'Who do you think you are to issue orders in this town? This man murdered one of our ranch crew yesterday when he was riding peacefully down by the river. Pol Glendale named Charlie Ute with his dying breath.'

Walt paused, gazed around the assembly to assure himself that he had their attention. 'If Pol Glendale is the man who shot Brad Edmond in the back with a shotgun, then you've got the wrong man. I shot him, and if he's since died, then I killed him.'

A stunned silence gripped those standing around when they heard Walt's admission. It was Rex Coulter, of course, who was first to find his voice. Realizing that this was the man he'd labelled a gun-slinger, a hired gun, he knew he had to get rid of him before he disclosed the events that had taken place at the Edmond ranch. 'Then you should be standing on that barrel,' he shouted, waving an arm, trying to encourage support for his assertion.

But there was little response, and the judge,

sensing an opportunity to restore some kind of order in the town, stepped forwards.

'I'm Samuel Hawkins,' he told Walt. 'Did I hear you aright, young man,' he said, 'has Brad Edmond been shot?'

'Brad Edmond is dead, Mr Hawkins. I witnessed his slaughter at the hands of the man called Pol Glendale.'

Judge Hawkins spoke over the murmurs of surprise and sympathy. 'I think you'd better step down from your horse and tell us what you know.' He gestured towards Charlie, 'And get that man down and bring him along. We'll hold a hearing in the Running Steer.'

When all the tables and chairs in the Running Steer were pushed aside, the vacant space was quickly filled with those eager to hear the details of the recent killings. Despite his portly frame, Judge Hawkins had somehow levered himself on to the long, polished counter where he could see and be seen by all.

'Now suppose you tell us what you saw yesterday,' he said to Walt, after banging on the counter with a bottle in order to gain everyone's attention.

Succinctly, Walt gave his evidence, told how one man had ridden up behind another and fired one barrel of his shotgun into his back. 'If I hadn't yelled, he would have put the contents of the other barrel into his victim, too.'

'What did he do when you let him know he'd been seen?' the judge wanted to know.

'He fired at me but I was too far away for it to have any effect.'

'What did you do?'

'I shot him. It seemed probable that when his shotgun had proved ineffective he'd try with his rifle or six-gun.'

'Did you hit him?'

'I did, but I didn't know until later that night that he'd died.'

'You're claiming self-defence?'

'I wasn't going to let him shoot me dead. His ruthlessness was apparent by the manner in which he'd attacked Mr Edmond.'

'You knew the identity of the shot man?'

'Not until I got him back to his home.'

'How did you know where he lived, if he was a stranger to you?'

Walt indicated the scrawny Ute who, with hands still tied behind his back, had been brought into the saloon. 'Charlie Ute had witnessed the shooting in the hills. He helped me to get Mr Edmond on to a horse and guided me to the ranch house. Charlie did his best to save Mr Edmond's life, and went to fetch the doctor while I stayed with the dying man and his daughter.'

'Pack of lies,' Rex Coulter shouted. 'Are you going to take the word of a hired gun?'

'The men who attacked Mr Edmond's home called me a hired killer, too. Were you among them?'

Rex Coulter didn't answer, but Judge Hawkins seized on Walt's comment.

'The Edmond place was attacked?' he asked.

'In darkness. Without warning and with murder on the minds of those who came.'

'We were there to arrest the men who'd killed Pol Glendale.'

'You came with blazing guns and burning fire brands, reckless of the life of a young woman who was mourning her dead father.'

'No one knew Brad Edmond was dead.'

'You could have broken off the attack when I told you he was. Instead you attempted to torch the building, knowing his daughter was inside.'

'No one intended to hurt the girl.'

'The dozens of bullets that shattered windows and are embedded in the walls tell a different story,' Walt accused, 'and the burned walls are testimony to your intention to kill her.'

'Is young Cassie OK?' asked Judge Hawkins.

'She's preparing to bury a murdered father,' he said, implying that in such circumstances the question ought not to have been posed, 'but she's alive.'

'Not everyone survived,' Rex Coulter muttered. 'You killed men, and the town wants justice for their deaths.'

'Mr Edmond was killed, too,' Walt responded.

Hoping to get the townspeople on his side, Rex reverted to the lies he'd previously voiced. 'Brad Edmond was trying to ruin Mr Stuart and brought in a hired gun to do it.'

'I'm not a hired gun. I fought because there was no other option.'

'For a man who claims that his gun isn't for hire you sure know how to use one. You've killed two men, put a bullet in the shoulder of another, and all but taken away Chuck Morrison's sight.'

Rex Coulter's exhortations were beginning to sway those gathered inside the Running Steer, but Doctor Cairns began to shoulder his way through the now murmuring crowd. He was carrying two long guns and put them on the long counter beside the sitting judge.

'Samuel,' he said, 'if this is some sort of trial then I think in the interest of justice you need to hear what I've got to say.'

Judge Hawkins gave a solemn nod then banged the bottle on the counter to put an end to the growing noise. 'Go ahead, John. The floor is yours.'

The doctor looked weary and unkempt, the result of more than thirty-six hours without sleep or a proper meal. He rubbed his eyes before addressing the assembly.

'Last night I was summoned to the Carter place, and when I got home I found Charlie Ute waiting for me. According to my wife he'd been outside the house most of the night, so I figured his errand was a matter of some urgency. He took me to Brad Edmond's place but I was too late. Brad was dead. Shot in the back, and the concentration of pellets proved that his assailant had fired at very close range.'

Several angry voices arose from the crowd. Even though Walt Ridgeway had already described the attack on Brad Edmond it needed one of their own citizens to confirm the truth of the matter. Nobody liked a back-shooter, and in this instance their repugnance was increased by the weapon used. Eyes were turned towards Rex Coulter, questioning his defence of Pol Glendale's actions, even if he was working for High Hill.

'When I got to the Edmond ranch,' John Cairns continued, 'it was clear that some kind of gun battle had taken place there and the house was still smouldering from an attempt to burn it down. Brad Edmond was dead, his daughter, Cassie, was shaken by the vicious attack on her home, and this young man,' he indicated Walt Ridgeway, 'was exhausted and smeared by his efforts to save the house from destruction. In my opinion, neither he nor Cassie were in any doubt that they were meant to die in the attack.'

'Do you know the reason behind the attack, John?' Judge Hawkins asked.

The doctor shook his head. 'I don't think the young couple can supply an answer to that question, but I took the long trail back to town along the riverside to examine the place where Brad Edmond had been shot. I found these.' He lifted the two guns off the counter and held them aloft for all to see. 'This one,' he said, giving preference to the rifle, 'has the initials BE burned into the stock. Brad Edmond,' he explained to make sure that everyone understood the significance. 'It hasn't been fired in a coon's age. The other one . . .' he waved the shotgun above his head, holding the barrels so that everyone could see the patterned inlay in the stock, '. . . this weapon, I believe, is familiar to most people here. Pol Glendale carried it everywhere he went. There are two discharged cartridges in the breech. The contents of one ended up in Brad Edmond's back.'

'That seems to bear out this fellow's story.' The judge's assessment found general favour with the men in the room.

'That's the way I see it,' agreed the doctor, 'and all the evidence I've seen so far lends the truth to everything he's told us. I believe that we owe this man and Charlie Ute a debt of gratitude for the way they tried to help Brad Edmond and his daughter.'

Nods of agreement occurred all around the room, and the earlier notion to lynch the old Ute was conveniently forgotten.

Once more, the judge used the bottle to gain everyone's attention. 'There are matters arising from this incident that require further investigation,' he said. 'When Sheriff Hayes returns to town I'll instruct him to get to the bottom of the matter. Rex Coulter, make yourself available to answer the sheriff's questions, because you seem to have significant knowledge that might provide us with an explanation for yesterday's occurrence.'

Rex Coulter looked uneasy. Thirty minutes earlier he'd believed that by inciting the town against Charlie Ute he would have diverted interest away from the killing of Brad Edmond and the attack on his ranch. Jonathan Barclay would buy the ranch from the daughter, and interest in that family would die forever when she left town. But that stranger had interfered again, turning everything upside-down.

The judge was telling Walt that he, too, would have to talk with Sheriff Hayes before leaving town. 'You haven't given your name,' he said, 'nor stated your business here in Elkhill.

'My name is Walt Ridgeway. I hold the rank of captain in the 9th Cavalry unit stationed at Fort Bridger in the Wyoming Territory.'

Even while he was uttering the last few words it was obvious that his name had had an effect on some of those present, including Doctor Cairns and Judge Hawkins. However, no one was more interested in the stranger's name than Rex Coulter. He didn't yet know how he would benefit from the information, but he was certain that he would. Perhaps all was not lost.

Walt was still speaking. 'I've come to Elkhill for a wedding,' he explained. 'Mine.'

'That might be difficult now,' Rex Coulter told him. 'The man you killed last night was Ezra Stuart, your bride-to-be's father.'

Moments after Rex Coulter's startling revelation, the saloon began to empty and the barman began to rearrange the tables and chairs in the big room. Those people who had interrupted their business to be abreast of events in the town now went on their way, eager to spread the story to others. Judge Hawkins and Doctor Cairns remained, staying close to Walt Ridgeway as though certain that he was some kind of magnet capable of attracting all manner of incidents and trouble. Jonathan Barclay, having watched the failed lynching from the safety of his office, had rushed across the street to learn first-hand the meaning of the assembly, and lingered close at hand. As a fellow member of the legal profession, Judge Hawkins felt beholden to introduce him to Walt Ridgeway.

The four men had gathered around one of the repositioned tables with shots of whiskey when the batwings were brushed aside by a big-shouldered man who wore a grim expression on his face and a star on his chest. Andy Hayes stalked across to the table around which the others were gathered, and gave each a questioning look.

'I leave town for half a day and I come back to a spate of killings.'

His glare took on greater intensity when he studied Walt Ridgeway. 'If the story I've been told is true, then you must be the fellow who killed Ezra Stuart. That won't make you a popular man around here.'

At that moment, his general popularity in and around Elkhill wasn't Walt's main concern. Nor was the fact that the previous day's incidents had shattered forever the high reputation of Ezra Stuart, who had been regarded as an honest and judicious man. For several hours, Walt had been aware that High Hill riders had been involved in the raid on the Edmond ranch, but not for one moment had he considered it probable that the owner himself had been involved in such a cowardly attack. Walt, however, wasn't interested in finding a motive for Ezra Stuart's behaviour – his death had a more fundamental effect on his own life.

Walt had met Connie Stuart almost two years earlier, introduced by the wife of a fellow officer with whom she'd been staying in Fort Collins. Their mutual attraction had grown over the course of several meetings, and was pushed to a head by his own posting to Fort Bridger and his friend's posting to the South West Territories. His offer of marriage had been accepted, and he was currently on a month's furlough to finalize the matter. Although it would be a drastic change to the life-style to which she was currently accustomed, it had been agreed that Connie would join him in married quarters at Fort Bridger. Now, the circumstances surrounding her father's death would make their next meeting a difficult occasion.

For the sheriff's benefit, Walt repeated his story. Andy Hayes wanted to know if he could identify anyone involved.

'It was too dark to see faces,' he said.

'What about earlier, down by the river?'

Walt shook his head. 'The only person I saw was the killer, but Charlie Ute saw other men working in another part of the river.'

'Doing what?' asked the sheriff.

'Panning for gold, I suspect,' Walt said, 'but they're wasting their time. I commanded the troop that escorted surveyors in those hills last year. They might hold other minerals, but there's no gold – and if there's no gold in the hills, it can't be washed down in the streams.'

When Sheriff Hayes asked the others if they'd heard any rumours about gold he received head shakes all round.

'Perhaps the bucko who tried to hang Charlie Ute can throw some light on the matter,' suggested Walt. 'He seems to be well informed about the other matter.'

'Rex Coulter,' supplied Judge Hawkins, 'the High Hill foreman.'

EIGHT

When he returned to his office, Jonathan Barclay found Rex Coulter waiting for him. 'What are you doing here?' he asked, with more than a hint of annoyance. 'The sheriff is looking for you, and I don't want him to find you with me. He's not a fool. I don't want him to suspect any connection between us.'

'You mean you want it to seem like your hands are clean, but it doesn't matter about me.'

'I mean that if you stick to your story and claim you were obeying the orders of your boss who was protecting his land, then you'll be absolved of blame. Cattlemen have always done their own fighting in this country. On the other hand, any connection we have now will look suspicious when I'm the owner of a ranch that becomes suddenly wealthy. Only come here when I send for you.'

Rex had never liked the lawyer's manner, always talking down at him as though he wasn't suitable to share the same room. Ezra Stuart had been his employer for ten years, with wealth that far outweighed Jonathan Barclay's, but in ranching matters they'd always conversed as equals, the boss aware of the abilities of the men he hired. For now, the ranch foreman shrugged his shoulders – when the scheme was realized he'd take his share and they wouldn't need to speak to each other again.

'Still,' he said, the coincidence of the event too great to pass without comment, 'who would have suspected that the interfering stranger would turn out to be Connie Stuart's soldier boy.' He smirked. He'd watched her grow, seen her tomboyish teenage years change into chin-lifted vanity, but it hadn't removed a desire for her that had never seemed possible to fulfil. Yet now perhaps there was hope. Not only did she need him to manage the ranch, but he was on the threshold of shattering her dreams of bliss. He could hardly wait to tell her that the man she hoped to marry was the man who had killed her father.

'That man could be dangerous to our plans,' Jonathan Barclay stated, pleased when his words wiped the smile from the other's face.

'What do you mean?'

'He knows there's no gold in the river, but he's aware of other minerals in the hills. We don't want him reaching conclusions that aren't good for us.'

'You want me to do something about it?'

'Not yet, we don't want to do anything that will bring army investigators to Elkhill. Besides, it might not be necessary.'

'What do you mean?'

'If there isn't a wedding he'll return to the Wyoming territory and we won't hear from him again. That would be best for everyone.'

Rex Coulter left the lawyer's office through the rear door, and taking care not to be seen, used a circuitous route to Reno's Retreat where Frankie Teal and Tex had resettled their weary bodies against the long bar. Rex drew them aside and all three gathered their horses and returned to the High Hill ranch house.

Three hours later Walt Ridgeway followed the same trail. He'd rented a hotel room and spruced himself up with lather, razor and clean clothes before making the journey to the home of his intended bride. It had been his intention to have a night's rest in a proper bed before presenting himself at High Hill, but circumstances demanded a change to that plan. Connie, he guessed, would have been told of his involvement in her father's death, so it was imperative to talk to her as soon as possible. It wouldn't be an easy meeting, certainly not one brimming with the eager tenderness he'd been anticipating since leaving Fort Bridger several days earlier, but that made it all the more important that it took place speedily.

The sun's final light of the day was sending long shadows across the compound when Walt rode through the tall gate at High Hill. His arrival didn't go unobserved, and half-a-dozen men were at his back when he left his horse at a rail and headed for the house. He was five steps away when the abrupt opening of the door brought him to a halt.

Unsurprisingly, Connie Stuart was dressed in black when she stepped outside. Long black skirt, black blouse that was buttoned to the throat and a black ribbon tying back her hair, the contrast making it more startlingly blonde than Walt remembered. He looked at her from the foot of the steps that led up to the long veranda on which she stood. He hadn't been expecting smiles and warm greetings when he arrived, but nor had he expected the visage of cold hatred she presented to him. Nor the rifle that was cushioned against her shoulder and pointed at him with obvious intent. Her eyes were narrowed so that they almost obscured the dullness imposed on them by sadness; her lips moved slightly as though she had words to utter but none came.

They gazed at each other for several moments before Walt spoke. 'There's no need for that,' he said, indicating the rifle.

'Perhaps you think I don't know how to use it,' she said, her voice rasping with emotion, 'or that I won't use it.' The finger within the guard began to tighten around the trigger.

'I came here to talk,' Walt said.

'You killed my father. I don't think there's anything else to say.'

'I had no other choice,' Walt told her. 'He led an attack on another man's home which was meant to kill everyone inside. Including me. I had to fight back.'

'Liar,' she yelled at him. 'Brad Edmond was trying to ruin us and my father wanted to know why. But you answered his questions with bullets and I've got a longing to give you the same medicine.'

'Connie,' Walt began, but she interrupted before he could continue.

'Miss Stuart,' she snapped at him. 'Any familiarity we might once have had is now dead. You will be, too, if you don't get off my land. If you're found on it again you'll be killed.'

'Why wait?' The voice asking the question, posing the threat, belonged to a man who had emerged from the house with Connie, but who had lingered in the shadows until now. Rex Coulter stepped forward, a hand resting on the butt of the pistol worn on his right hip.

Connie shook her head and turned dismissively, intending to return indoors.

Walt wasn't prepared to let it end without another effort to convince her of the truth.

'I don't think Brad Edmond was planning to divert the water away from your range,' he said. 'He was killed because he confronted some men panning for gold on his property.'

'Good luck to them,' she said. 'I hope they overrun his range, destroy his herd and leave his family to die in poverty.'

'That's a bitter wish for a daughter whose father, like yours, has just been killed.'

'I reckon he's got some interest in that girl,' Rex Coulter butted in, adding with innuendo, 'the pair of them all alone in her ranch house last night.'

Affronted by the suggestion, Walt began to climb the steps, intent upon grappling with the speaker. Connie Stuart put a stop to his advance, hefting the rifle that had never left her shoulder with menace.

'Get back into the dirt of the yard,' she told him. 'Cassie Edmond can have you. As far as I'm concerned you are murderers together. Now get on your horse and don't ever come back here.'

Walt paused for only a moment. The hard lines around her mouth and the dark anger that glinted in her eyes made it clear that Connie Stuart's mind was set and there were no words capable of changing it. When Rex Coulter eased past his new employer and made his way down the steps, Walt knew there was little to be achieved by hanging around. If a gun, held in the hands of a woman who seemed eager to use it against him, hadn't been pointed in his direction he might have retaliated against the foreman's slur against not only his own character, but that of Cassie Edmond, too. The grin worn by Rex Coulter was almost enough for Walt to throw caution aside, but he turned around and began to walk towards the rail where he'd hitched his horse. He heard the house door close and knew that Connie had gone indoors.

'You left town too quickly,' he told Rex Coulter as they walked side by side. 'The sheriff wants to hear your version of the attack on Brad Edmond's home.'

'What's to tell,' he said, 'I wasn't there. I don't think it ever happened. You probably started the fire yourself as part of some crazy plan to cover up the murder of Mr Stuart.' He guffawed at Walt's incredulity. 'What you've got to remember, soldier boy, is that this is cattle country. The most powerful people in the territory make the laws here, and that just happens to be High Hill.'

Those who had been gathered at the foot of the veranda steps were now following close behind as though they sensed that Connie's departure did not mark the end of the episode. One or two chuckled at the foreman's remark, but without humour. Ahead of Walt, a youngish cowboy waited by the yard gate, which had been closed since his arrival. His face and the twitchy movement of hands that had no particular task to engage them, were marks of nervousness, as though he wished he were far away from this place, nursing cows on High Hill's most remote pasture.

Another man was untying Walt's horse from the rail. There was no nervousness in the way he proffered the reins that he held in his left hand, just a meanness in his eyes, and a twist of his shoulders made obvious to Walt that his right arm was held across his chest in a linen sling. Walt guessed that this man had got in the way of his bullets and wanted revenge in any manner possible.

'Don't forget what Miss Stuart told you,' Rex reminded Walt as took the reins, 'you're a dead man if you come back here.'

Walt's glare carried a promise that this wouldn't be the last time the two of them would meet. For now, however, the odds were stacked too highly against him, and it was time for the bugler to blow recall, time to reassess the situation. He put his hands on the saddle horn, and lifted his left foot into the stirrup in order to mount up. But he didn't make it into the seat of the saddle: it twisted and slid across the horse's back, pitching Walt on to the ground.

It wasn't necessary for anyone to explain the reason for his fall. The cinch keeping the saddle in place had been untied, and it had fallen away from his mount as soon as the stirrup had been asked to take his full weight. All around there were calls of derision, mockery and sniggering at Walt's ungainly tumble.

'What chance have we of protection from the Sioux when the soldier boys aren't even able to climb on their horses?' asked Rex Coulter. Catcalls and jeers greeted the taunt. 'Help the poor man to his feet.'

'I don't need any help.'

'Sure you do. Just because you killed our boss doesn't mean we can't give you a helping hand. Frankie.'

Frankie Teal stepped forward, but he didn't offer his hand. 'Get up,' he growled, then kicked out violently, the hard toecap of his high-boot crashing into Walt's ribs.

Walt grunted and twisted in an effort to avoid the next kick that was aimed at him. He tried to roll under the belly of his horse but someone had grabbed its bridle and was leading it away so that he was exposed to their violent intentions. Kicks pounded his body, front and back. His initial thoughts to fight back were soon abandoned. He tried to use his arms to ward away the booted blows but they were an ineffectual defence. From his position on the ground, it was impossible to generate the necessary strength to repel the onslaught. Within seconds, his arms had ceased to be a weapon with which to fight back and had become nothing more than a cover for his head. He curled his body, brought his knees up to his chest and shrunk his head into his shoulders, but boots and fists were battering every part of his exposed frame. When the beating stopped, Walt was unconscious.

It was with a great deal of reluctance that Rex Coulter called a halt to the onslaught. He wouldn't have been upset if Walt Ridgeway had been killed – the man had become an uneasy itch in his mind. The way he looked at him seemed to threaten a reckoning to come, but if he was going to kill him it would be best done without witnesses. His body could be dumped in the river or some remote spot in the hills and forgotten about – but Jonathan Barclay had warned against that. The army, he'd suggested, might come looking for a missing officer. Rex wasn't prepared to do anything that would put at risk the success of their scheme – money was more important than scratching an itch.

Everyone else was satisfied that Walt Ridgeway would be anxious to leave the territory. He had nothing to stay for except similar treatment at their hands. His saddle was refastened and he was slung across his horse. His bound hands were tied to one stirrup and his bound feet to the other. Larry Grimes was pressed into service to lead the horse away from High Hill, into the high country where someone would eventually find it and release its battered load.

From the window of her house, Connie Stuart coldly watched the entire affair.

NINE

Two years a cow-hand at High Hill had tutored Larry Grimes into carrying out the foreman's orders without question. This day, although he still gave voice to the objection that burned within, he left the yard reluctantly, towing in his wake the bay with the stamp of the US Cavalry on its rump and the bound and unconscious figure hanging over its saddle. Rex Coulter had boasted that the cattlemen made the laws in this territory, but Larry wasn't sure that Sheriff Hayes shared that view. He would have some explaining to do if he ran into that lawman before reaching the high ground, and he doubted his ability to come up with a convincing reason for toting around a busted-up army officer. The main problem was that he couldn't justify the situation to himself, so how could he hope to convince anyone else of his innocence?

Early talk of gold had excited Larry and his head had been filled with dreams of riches, which had not been diminished by Rex's warning that their hard labour in the river had to be undertaken in addition to their normal ranch work. They needed to work in secret if they weren't to alert others to the wealth that was to be had – and also because they were trespassing on another man's land. However, he'd promised that the rewards would change their lives forever. The prospect of heavy labour hadn't deterred Larry, and the fact that the gold rightly belonged to another was a thought easily pushed aside. A man had to take his opportunities when they arose – and how could it be called stealing if a man was ignorant of what he owned?

It was Rex's attitude towards Brad Edmond, however, that made Larry uneasy. To him, it made more sense to avoid the rancher, but Rex had taken to goading him at every opportunity. It seemed as though he was looking for a fight, and despite Rex's account of yesterday's events, Pol Glendale had followed Brad Edmond with the express purpose of killing him. Rex had lied, too, to Mr Stuart, and it was the foreman, not the owner, who had ordered the attack on the Edmond ranch. In Larry's opinion, the burning of the building had been an unnecessary act. Clearly, Rex was prepared to kill to get the gold – he was driven by the prospect of wealth, and hadn't shown a moment's remorse over the death of his former employer.

Larry looked back at the man slung over the trailing horse. He was motionless, still unconscious, lucky to be alive. Rex's lies and aggression had led to further trouble. Not only had her father been killed, but Miss Connie had now been driven apart from the man she had intended marrying. He recalled her standing on the veranda with the rifle hoisted against her shoulder. All of her willpower, it seemed, had been needed to prevent her squeezing the trigger, but so tense had she been that he'd suspected the smallest involuntary tremble would have undone her effort. Now that man was in his care, and he wanted rid of the responsibility as quickly as possible. He would leave him somewhere close to the river trail, which was the most used route in and out of Elkhill.

With his mind thus occupied he rode south, using every patch of woodland and sunken gulley that helped to keep his journey a secret affair. Every stretch of open meadow land he approached nervously, casting glances all around and stopping occasionally to listen for any sound that might herald approaching riders. It wasn't until he'd reached the low hills, still a couple of miles short of the recognized trail, that his courage deserted him. The high ground should have been a place of greater concealment, but from the moment he entered the tight little valley he was convinced that he was under observation.

For quarter of a mile he rode, his eyes seeking high and low for any sign that would confirm his suspicion. None was forthcoming, but his mind was no less eased. Fearing that all blame for the recent events would fall on his shoulders if he were found with the hog-tied soldier, he sent the bay running ahead through the valley while he turned tail and beat a hasty retreat back to High Hill. He didn't ease his pace until the tall ranch gates came into sight.

Before heading for Elkhill, Rex Coulter had spoken to Connie Stuart. The soldier-boy wouldn't trouble her again, he'd told her, letting her know that not only was her ranch in capable hands, but that he was also offering her his personal protection. She'd made it clear that she understood his meaning, but without any indication that she was either accepting or rejecting his interest.

'Did you kill him?' was all she'd asked, and had merely nodded when Rex told her that Walt Ridgeway was probably scurrying back to Fort Bridger as quickly as he could.

Then, self-satisfied, certain that his plans would be fulfilled, and that with careful handling a wealthy future could be his, he'd ridden into town.

Hitching his mount outside the Running Steer, he could see a light burning in the lawyer's office on the other side of the street. Jonathan Barclay had been adamant that the foreman should only go there when summoned, so he stepped up on to the boards and headed for the saloon's swing doors. A man ambling in the same direction called his name.

'Is that you, Rex Coulter?' asked Sheriff Hayes. 'I want to talk to you about those killings.'

'Not much I can tell you, Sheriff.'

'Yet you instigated a lynching party. Tried to get Charlie Ute hanged.'

'Pol named him as his killer with his dying breath.

96

Him and the soldier-boy.'

'Captain Ridgeway tells a different story, one that's backed by evidence. He also says that a group of men were panning the river for gold. If that was you and others from High Hill, I can tell you that you're wasting your time. There's no gold there.'

'That the same Captain Ridgeway that killed Mr Stuart?'

'I still want to know what Mr Stuart was doing at the Edmond place?'

'Cow people fight their own battles, Sheriff. You've been here long enough to know that.'

'Those times are past, Rex. I'll be investigating this further. Make sure you're around when I come looking for you.'

Rex Coulter grinned at the lawman. 'I'm not going anywhere, Sheriff. No sir, I'm staying right here in Elkhill!'

Andy Hayes detected a hidden meaning in the rancher's words, but couldn't figure it out. With a final caution for the High Hill foreman, he moved further along the street towards Reno's Retreat. Scornfully, before stepping inside the Running Steer, Rex Coulter watched the departing lawman. A movement across the street at the window of Jonathan Barclay's office caught his eye. The lawyer was beckoning him, so he re-crossed the street. The whiskey celebration he'd promised himself would have to wait a little longer.

Jonathan Barclay was not alone. The other man was a stranger to Rex Coulter, but by his appearance it was clear that he had been travelling hard for a couple of days.

'We've got a problem,' the lawyer said, without troubling to introduce the men to each other. 'Johnny's come from Helena, rushed here to get ahead of tomorrow's stage. There'll be a government man on board, coming to announce the findings of the survey. Cassie Edmond will learn the value of her land.'

'The stage is due about four in the afternoon,' said Rex, 'you'll have to work quickly.'

'Don't be a fool,' Barclay snapped at him. 'No deal can be organized and ratified in that time.'

'Then what are we going to do?'

'I'll go out to the Edmond place tomorrow. Convince the girl that it's in her best interest to sell up. Meanwhile, you need to prevent the man from the Territorial Office reaching Elkhill. Permanently. By the time a replacement is sent out I should have everything tied up.'

'You want me to stop the stage? I've never done anything like that before,' said Rex.

'Can't be difficult,' said the lawyer. 'Men are doing it all the time. The sheriff's just come back to town after chasing a bunch. Everyone will think the same gang has struck again.'

'Yeah,' murmured Rex, 'and sometimes road agents get caught and hanged.'

Jonathan was less than sympathetic when he spoke again: 'Then make sure you're not one of them. You'll need to take a couple of your men with you.'

'I can't do that,' he replied. 'What argument could I use to convince them becoming highwaymen will help them to find gold? The recent killings have already shaken their determination to continue working the river, and they aren't going to be happy when word gets around that there never was any gold to find.'

'Can you do it alone?'

Rex looked doubtful.

Johnny Brassil spoke up. 'I'll ride with you,' he said. 'I was sent here to help. We all lose if the announcement is made before you have the deeds to the place in your pocket.'

So it was decided. Next day, Rex and Johnny would ride west of the river and find a suitable place to ambush the stagecoach from Helena.

Charlie Ute had recognized the trailing big bay horse the moment it entered the narrow valley. He'd worked horses, caught mustangs and traded them since his youth. He could judge them in an instant, knew those that were gentle and those with spirit. Picked out those that had never been shod nor saddled and those that had been schooled by the pony soldiers. The big bay was one of the latter.

The nervous antics of the man leading the bay had also been noted by Charlie. He'd followed and watched until the bay had been chased ahead and the rider had turned and fled as though all the spirits of Sitting Bull's ancestors were on his tail.

Charlie had descended to the floor of the valley

and set his paint to a long-striding lope in pursuit of the bay. The cavalry horse hadn't run far, its progress impeded by the loose, long lead rein that was in danger of becoming entangled with its forelegs. It waited patiently while Charlie dismounted and approached with an open hand. He rubbed its muzzle, then examined the figure tied across its back.

Walt's eyes were open now, although the area around the left one was badly discoloured. He groaned as Charlie cut away his bonds and lowered him to the ground. His body was a mass of pain – no place, he believed, was less sore than any other. Even sitting on the ground was a source of discomfort.

Eventually, however, he remounted his horse and followed Charlie, who cut a trail into the hills. They travelled slowly, but didn't stop until they reached a small, dilapidated cabin that clung tenaciously to the hillside. Walt had seen similar structures in the past, thrown up by men more eager to dig in the hillside than build robust dwelling places. Still, miraculously, some of them survived many years, this one included, with the comfort and protection little diminished from what it had provided when it was first built.

Few words had been uttered by the Ute since rescuing the cavalry officer, and his taciturnity continued when they were settled inside the shack. Yet Charlie kept busy, finding a salve for Walt to rub into his bruises, brewing coffee, then stabling the horses in a small fenced-off corral adjoining the building.

When he applied it, Walt reckoned that the salve had been prepared for the treatment of horses. It was an unpleasant shade of green and gave off an even more unpleasant smell. In addition, when it came into contact with those places where his skin had split, it caused a pain so severe that he judged it akin to a spear being thrust clean through to his innards. If speed of recovery was governed by intensity of agony then he reckoned he'd be healed by morning, but long into the night every movement induced further suffering.

TEN

Eventually, Walt had fallen asleep on Charlie's low bunk. When he awoke the room was bright with sunlight. He moved gingerly, and was surprised to discover he could do so with a great deal less discomfort than he had prepared himself for. Whatever ingredients the salve contained, they had prevented the bumps and abrasions from swelling further, and to some extent had repaired the tears in his skin. When he rubbed away the potion that had been applied to the particularly deep cut over his left eye he found the skin was dry and the gash closing up. He figured there would always be a scar, but that it was only superficial damage.

Even so, Walt's body resembled an old Navajo rug, discoloured as it was with splotches of purple, red, pink and yellow where the blows and kicks he'd taken were in varying stages of bruising. In several places the skin was tight and tender, but if he didn't make sudden or excessive movements he was able to get around the room unaided.

A more pressing matter was his clothing. In their current condition, torn and grubby with dirt and blood, his shirt and trousers were almost unwearable. Charlie had no implements capable of performing basic repairs to them, and Walt's other clothes were in his Elkhill hotel room. He was reluctant to return to town in such disarray, and could hardly expect Charlie to do the errand for him. The Ute had an even greater reason to give the place a wide berth, since on his last visit they had tried to hang him.

The only other people who might help him were Cassie Edmond and her crew. So, after a brief breakfast of coffee and beans, he draped an old grey blanket around his body and followed Charlie to the Edmond place. Out of necessity born of Walt's injuries and because Charlie scarcely demanded greater speed from his paint, it was a slow journey.

When they rode into the ranch yard they were met by Cy Cuttle and another man, both of them toting spades. The bruises on Walt's face were of interest to both men but neither spoke of them.

'Miss Cassie's indoors,' Cy told Walt, 'but it would be better to leave her for a few minutes. We've just put her pa in the ground.'

Walt scanned around noting the absence of neighbours.

'It's the way Miss Cassie wanted it,' Cy said, guessing the question that Walt was keeping to himself. 'She's a bit nervous of people coming to the house at the moment. Didn't even want the parson here. Said her own words when we lowered her pa into the hole.'

Walt liked that about the young woman – it showed a strong character. It couldn't have been an easy decision to make, and no doubt it would arouse a lot of gossip about sacrilegious behaviour in Elkhill, but she'd had her reasons for burying him on her own, and she'd stuck to them. He'd read over fallen soldiers himself, and didn't think the Good Lord would heed the words less because they'd been spoken by a soldier not a churchman. 'Perhaps we should ride on,' he said, 'come back tomorrow.'

'No. She'll be pleased to see you, and she wouldn't have turned you away if you'd been in time for the burial.' He handed his shovel to the other man before speaking again. 'Had one visitor before we got started.' It was clear from his tone that whoever it was hadn't met with his approval. The thought flashed through Walt's mind that it might have been Connie Stuart. Cassie didn't need that bitter woman throwing wrong-minded accusations at her, neither about the death of their respective fathers nor tawdry insinuations about his time with her. But when Cy spoke again he dispelled any suspicion that Cassie's visitor had been his prospective bride. 'She should have chased him off with a load of buckshot,' he grumbled, then quickly realized that not only was it not fitting to discuss his employer's affairs in such a manner, but on this morning, he'd used a particularly inappropriate expression. 'Well, let's grab some coffee in the bunkhouse before Lou and I set about our chores,' he added. He looked up at the old Ute on the droop-headed paint. 'You too, Charlie. We're obliged for what you did for Mr Edmond.'

The thought of someone upsetting Cassie Edmond rankled with Walt, but he refrained from pressing Cy Cuttle for more details. Trying to discover the identity of the previous visitor might be regarded as interfering in business that wasn't his concern, besides which, the older man was already embarrassed by his unguarded words. However, Cassie Edmond came out of the house while they were still in conversation.

The smile that began when she recognized Walt Ridgeway swiftly disappeared when she saw the damage to his face. She didn't share Cy Cuttle's reluctance to ask questions. She wanted to know what had happened, and everyone went into the house to listen while Walt related the previous day's events in Elkhill and at High Hill. When the telling was completed, Charlie Ute quit the ranch to return to his own shack in the hills, and Cy and Lou went back to their interrupted tasks.

Although Charlie Ute's medicine had been more effective than he had had any reason to expect, Walt still didn't object when Cassie offered to clean the wounds on his face and dab on turpentine, which had been locally promoted as an antiseptic. Unlike Charlie's potion, it didn't burn and cause pain when applied, but he still sucked in air as though her smallest touch was causing agony. Cassie knew he was teasing her and nudged him with an elbow to let him know she wasn't fooled. That touch, however, produced a genuine grunt of pain, and when persuaded to remove his shirt and the vast area of bruising was revealed, a fresh wave of concern for her patient swept over Cassie. Walt had said there had been a fight at High Hill which had led her to believe he'd been in a fist fight with a single opponent, but the marks on his body made that unlikely.

As she applied a tincture of arnica to the discoloured areas she wondered at his self-discipline. He'd been kicked and pounded relentlessly, and yet sat at her table seeking neither sympathy nor revenge. In addition, the woman he'd come to marry had had some involvement in the beating, its instigator if not an active participant. She realized that going to the aid of her father had cost him his marriage. She couldn't help wondering how much he regretted his efforts to help her father, and whether he harboured any portion of blame against her for the consequences he'd suffered. She looked up and found his eyes upon her.

With her hair swept behind her ears he'd become aware of her elfin prettiness. He'd been watching her face, noting the small care lines that creased her brow from time to time, and how her dark eyes reflected compassion for his suffering. Yet that compassion didn't totally hide from his observation her troubled thoughts. When she looked up her cheeks coloured slightly, not only to find herself under his study but also because she was aware that being alone with him in these circumstances gave rise to an element of impropriety. He was a stranger, a man of whom she knew little, yet from the first moment of meeting she had been comfortable with his presence. She didn't stop her administrations.

'We'd heard that Connie was to be married,' she said. 'Will you try again with her?'

'No.' Walt's answer was emphatic. 'I can understand her anger over the killing of her father, but she wasn't even prepared to listen to my version of events. And she could have stopped this,' he indicated the damage to his torso, 'with a single word. She didn't, and I reckon she wasn't kidding when she said she'd have me killed if I turned up there again. You need to know that she made some nasty remarks about me being alone with you the night your father died. There might be some gossip about it in town. When Cy told me you'd had an unwelcome visitor this morning I thought it might have been her.'

'That was Jonathan Barclay,' she said.

Walt recalled the name. 'The lawyer.'

'Said he was representing someone who wanted to make an offer for the ranch. Told me it would relieve me of all cares and make it possible for me to live comfortably in more civilized surroundings.'

'Is that what you want?'

'I don't know, my father is fresh buried. I haven't yet given any thought to my future. Don't know anything other than living on this ranch.'

'You need to discuss it with someone you trust,' Walt told her.

'What would you advise?' she asked.

Walt Ridgeway wasn't reluctant to help Cassie, but didn't know any details of her circumstances. There would be assets and liabilities attached to the ranch to take into consideration, but Cassie's own wishes and abilities were important, too. Cy Cuttle's opinion could be important to her – he would know the value of the current herd, and probably had knowledge of the schemes her father had planned for the future. Perhaps she needed to talk to someone at the bank, too. 'Take your time,' he told her. 'There's no need to make a snap decision.'

'Jonathan Barclay said he would be back for my answer tomorrow. That I should take the offer before it's withdrawn. He said a ranch soon begins to lose money if it isn't properly managed.'

If Cy Cuttle had overheard the lawyer's attempts to browbeat Cassie Edmond, then Walt well understood his anger. Whether or not Jonathan Barclay had arrived on the morning Brad Edmond was being buried, his manner had been high-handed and unnecessary. The mind of the dead man's daughter had been thrown into turmoil over a matter that needed time and calm consideration to resolve. 'Cy Cuttle seems capable of running things for a while, and if necessary you could hire an extra hand, but if you mean to stay here you'll probably have to sort out details of the current mortgage with the bank.'

Cassie's silence indicated her realization that she would be faced with many unfamiliar aspects of running a ranch if she was to stay. Her eyes remained fixed on Walt's and he understood the dilemma with which she was struggling.

'This place is your home,' he said, 'you don't have

to sell it. Perhaps sometime in the future you'll decide for yourself that you want to move away, but you don't have to make that decision immediately.'

'What should I tell Jonathan Barclay when he returns?'

'That the ranch isn't for sale. Keep Cy close while the lawyer's here.'

'Cy and Lou need to get back to the line cabin. They won't be here in the morning.'

Those words disheartened Walt for more than one reason. 'I was hoping one of them would collect my gear from the hotel. I don't want to ride into town in these ragged clothes.'

'Perhaps something belonging to my father will fit you,' Cassie suggested, after agreeing that Walt's shirt and trousers were beyond repair.

He accepted the offer and emerged from her father's room several minutes later wearing a plain blue wool shirt and some black pants that needed a belt to gather them tightly at the waist, but whose shortness in the leg was obscured by his shin-high boots.

'What will you do now,' asked Cassie, 'now that you and Connie. . . ?'

'Return to Fort Bridger.'

'Immediately?' Cassie was examining the bruises and abrasions that showed on his face, silently suggesting that he might want to wait until they'd disappeared.

'The alternative is to hang around Elkhill. I'm not sure that anyone there wants my company.' He offered a grin.

'You could stay here for a few days,' she said, the words coming out a little more quickly than she'd intended, as though uttering them while she had the courage to do so. 'I owe you some hospitality for trying to help my father and beating off the attack.' When he didn't immediately reply, she added, 'Of course, it would also mean that you'd be here in the morning when Jonathan Barclay calls.'

'I have to go into Elkhill for the belongings I left in the hotel,' he said. 'I thought I might deliver a message from you while I was there. Make it clear to Jonathan Barclay that he would be wasting his time coming out here tomorrow.'

'Would you do that?' she asked, her eyes widening and brightening as she looked at him.

'Of course.'

'You could still come back here,' she told him.

'I know very little about cattle,' he told her, 'but I suppose there'll be other jobs I can do.'

'Good,' she said and the slight smile that made her face glow was still in evidence when, gingerly, he climbed into the saddle and rode out of the yard towards Elkhill.

ELEVEN

Two full mail sacks were snug in the boot below the driver's feet when the Helena stagecoach hurried out of Hardin on its way to Lame Deer. It was the leg of the journey that passed through Elkhill. It carried no strongbox yet, due to the spate of recent robberies; a guard sat alongside the driver with his rifle lying in readiness across his knees. Inside, three passengers chatted amiably as the vehicle rolled and bounced in and out of the time-formed ruts. The day was warm and they were well on schedule. There had been no mishaps, no swollen river crossings to cause delays, or high country detours that over-exerted the team. Another five miles would bring them to the river crossing which preceded the ten-mile run into Elkhill, where hospitality awaited the passengers and a fresh team would be coupled to the coach.

Buckskin Bob had his team running in harmony, striding with measured regularity so that the motion of the coach caused the least possible discomfort to the passengers. People said he had more empathy with horses than he had with his own kind, and his way with horses had kept him employed all his adult life. None of them had ever tried to cheat him at the card-table, bum drinks from him or try to woo away the women he'd known. All of those accusations, however, he could place at the door of the man sitting on the box beside him.

'Grubber' George Payton had always had more to say for himself than his pal Buckskin, and it was that talkativeness that was usually at the root of the scrapes and minor misadventures that had dogged his life. If there had been times when he'd leant on friendship to see him through tricky periods then he squared it by assuring himself that if the situations were reversed he wouldn't deny his last penny to any friend. To Buckskin's knowledge and indignation, that was a claim that had never been put to the test. Most of the time, however, they rubbed along in the grouchy companionship they'd shared for many years.

Barely had the observation left Buckskin's mouth that the most likely hold-up area was behind them than Grubber thought he saw a movement among the bushes ahead. Within seconds, as they drew alongside that shrubbery, a rider emerged. A dark neckerchief covered the lower part of his face and he held a pistol in his hand.

'Halt that team,' yelled the masked man and he fired his gun in the air to add threat to his command.

'There's only one,' Buckskin shouted, 'I reckon we can outrun him.'

112

As he cracked the whip over the heads of the lead horses and yelled for more pace, the hold-up man fired his gun again. If he was surprised when the driver ignored his command he was even more taken aback by the speed of the guard's response. A bullet from Grubber's rifle flew close to his head and flicked away part of the brim of his hat. He fired again, twice, the lead flying high into the sky, untroublesome to the men on the high seat. Another bullet whizzed past his own head, which extracted a mean curse before he jabbed his spurs into the flanks of his horse and hurried in pursuit of the fleeing coach.

Grubber pushed aside a couple of bags so that he was almost lying flat along the roof of the coach as he tried to get a telling shot at the chasing bandit. Marksmanship had been an essential skill when he'd been employed as a hunter supplying meat to the gangs building the Union Pacific railroad, and he'd retained it throughout his life. In those days, however, he'd been a static hunter waiting for the ideal moment to take down his unsuspecting quarry, but trying to draw a bead on this pursuer was a more difficult matter. Not only did he have a moving target to aim at, but he was being tossed and bounced so violently by the motion of the racing stagecoach that it was impossible to keep the target in his sights for more than a fraction of a second. Still, he fired shot after shot at the rider in his wake, sending them close enough to discourage the man from closing the gap.

'Keep 'em running, Bob,' Grubber shouted over his shoulder, 'I reckon he'll give up soon!' He fired another shot, causing the follower to swerve aside, almost pulling his horse to a halt. Grubber pulled the trigger again, but the metallic click it produced announced that he'd used up all the ammunition. He reached for his pocket, his fingers closing around some loose bullets with which he meant to reload the gun – but instead, a gunshot from the trail ahead and an accompanying grunt from his pal demanded his attention. Buckskin Bob had slumped forwards and was sliding into the footwell alongside the mail bags.

The reins had fallen from Bob's hands, allowing the horses to run free. Grubber's concern for his pal was forced to take second place to the task of gaining control of the team before disaster befell everyone. Leaving the rifle on the roof of the coach, he clambered back on to his seat and would have picked up the reins if a second shot hadn't rung out, the bullet hitting him between the shoulder blades. Involuntarily, his arms were flung wide and his body twisted. Deprived of all control of his body he tumbled backwards. He didn't hear the frantic cries of his passengers, didn't hear anything as he was dead when he hit the hard ground below.

The wild-eyed horses, startled by gunshots and released from the control to which they were accustomed, careered ahead, oblivious of the shouts and fears of the people inside the coach. Instinctively, they followed the trail that swung this way and that between trees and around boulders on its downhill course to the river. Five hundred yards had been covered before the threatened disaster occurred.

A wheel struck a huge embedded rock and the whole coach lifted off the ground. The force with which it landed not only caused damage to two wheels but also buckled the axle-tree and cracked one of the shafts. The pressure on the cracked shaft was too great to bear when they reached a bend in the trail. The shaft snapped completely, causing the vehicle to slew and crash sideways into a solid oak tree.

Two of the passengers, a man and his wife, died instantly. Already thrown to and fro as the coach hurtled, unchecked, along the uneven trail, her neck was broken by the whip-like manner in which her head was thrown from side to side by the sudden halt. Her husband was thrown against a jagged edge of shattered coachwork, impaling him, piercing him through to the heart.

The third passenger, dazed and shaken, pushed open the door and stumbled on to the road. His knees seemed incapable of bearing his weight as he tottered away from the smashed vehicle. He rubbed a hand across his brow, felt the lump that was forming, and winced at the pain it caused. Dizziness engulfed him, he needed to sit until it passed but his way was barred by a chestnut horse. Its rider's face was covered and the gun he held was pointed in his direction. Perhaps, when he found his voice, he really believed that stating he was on official business for the territory of Montana would carry sufficient weight to persuade the bandits to proceed no further with their attack and ride away without inflicting further violence upon him.

'My name is George Turnbull,' he announced, 'I'm on my way to Elkhill with an official document for that town's council.'

'Then I reckon you're just the man we're seeking,' said Rex Coulter who was beginning to regain his brutishness now that lumps of lead were no longer flying past his ears. 'Hand over the letter.'

'I will not,' said George Turnbull, summoning up every semblance of authority he could manage under the current constraints of pain and threat. He placed a hand over his coat where the envelope rested in an inner pocket.

It was then that he realized that a second man, dismounted, had joined them, and roughly thrust him against the damaged coach. George Turnbull's head struck the solid timber frame and stirred up the numerous pains that had been caused by the crash. When the man tried to pull open his coat to reach the secreted letter, George was still indignant enough to protest and struggle. His protests earned him an open-handed face slap followed by a punch into the pit of his stomach. He groaned, his knees bent and his body sagged and he would have fallen to the ground if Johnny Brassil hadn't held him upright long enough to be able to secure the letter. Then he allowed George Turnbull to slump on to the ground and cast his eyes over the long, stiff envelope that was sealed with the insignia of the Territory.

'I guess this is what Mr Barclay wants,' he told Rex Coulter as he stuffed it inside his shirt. 'Time to go.'

George Turnbull raised his head, made one further effort to impart his authority on the situation. 'You have no right to take that,' he proclaimed. 'I demand you return it to me.'

It was Rex Coulter who answered. 'This is the only thing you're getting,' he said, and fired his pistol twice. Either shot, one in the head and the other in the heart, would have been sufficient to kill the functionary.

Johnny Brassil climbed into the saddle and the pair rode away.

After leaving Cassie Edmond, Jonathan Barclay made another house call before returning to his office. Like the one he'd left behind, the second ranch was also a place in mourning and its new owner a young woman with fire in her eyes. This time, however, he knew that *he* wasn't the match that ignited them, and Connie Stuart made every effort to be hospitable to her unexpected visitor.

Connie had been on the long veranda when the lawyer's high-wheeled buggy rolled into the compound. Larry Grimes was with her, imparting news of a new-born foal. The ranch-hand stepped aside while his new employer greeted her caller, but waited at a discreet distance to continue their conversation after Jonathan Barclay's departure.

'I did a good deal of work on your father's behalf,' Barclay began after delivering his opening condolences, 'I hope I can be of service to you in the future.'

117

Connie's eyes flashed with anger. 'The best service you can do for me is to prosecute my father's killer in front of a hanging judge.'

'I understand your need for justice.' The lawyer's words were spoken gently.

'I should have killed him when I had him at the end of my rifle barrel.'

The words Jonathan Barclay next used were those that would have been uttered by any lawyer advocating the rule of law to resolve a problem, but there was something in his tone and the direct manner in which his eyes were fixed on her that told a different story. 'That would be the wrong thing to do. Sheriff Hayes would arrest you and you would go to prison. That's no place for a woman like you.'

'So why hasn't he arrested Walt Ridgeway? Why is that man still free?'

'Any prosecution at the moment would find him innocent because his account of the killing of Pol Glendale is corroborated by evidence given by Doctor Cairns.'

'What about my father whom he killed in cold blood?'

'His story is backed by the Edmond girl's testimony. At present, the truth can't be established – but who knows what will be discovered in the future. Perhaps a deeper investigation is needed. I'd be happy to organize it for you, Miss Stuart.'

Just as Rex Coulter's manner had, the previous day, alerted Connie to his desire for her, so, too, did

Jonathan Barclay's. Despite his controlled, dispassionate voice, something showed in his facial movements. He fixed her with a look of such intense scrutiny that it seemed as though he was trying to see the thoughts in her mind. It made his interest in her clearly something more than a lawyer and client relationship. She was less offended by it than she had been by her foreman's leering proposition. Jonathan Barclay was more debonair, his social status more acceptable than Rex Coulter, and his bearing depicted a man capable of achievement. He had the right sort of influence and contacts to get results. 'Can you succeed, Mr Barclay?' she'd asked. 'Will Walt Ridgeway be punished as he deserves to be?'

'Leave the matter in my hands,' he told her, a conspiratorial smile forming. 'One way or another I think Walt Ridgeway will get the punishment he deserves.'

On the drive back to Elkhill, Jonathan Barclay pondered over a future with Connie Stuart as his wife. He'd been quick to dismiss any interest in long-term possession of the Edmond place, which, as a cattle ranch, provided neither a quick nor an easy way to become rich. He was content to let Rex Coulter work his life away trying to build it into a thriving concern. Yet a man of great wealth, which he would become when he disposed of the rights to the copper deposits in the high ground of the Edmonds' land, needed a home of elegance and character, and High Hill was such an establishment. It was one of the top ranches in Montana, but, as owner, there would be no need to quit his law practice nor get his hands dirty nor his backside sore chasing cows. An experienced manager could be brought in to get the best from the crew, land and stock, and he, when married to Connie, would reap not only the profits but also the honour and respect that is always afforded to major landowners.

Perhaps, when he sold on the mineral rights, he would maintain a small interest, thereby connecting him with industry as well as ranching. The influence of such a man would be enormous, perhaps great enough to raise him to the position of governor when the Territory gained statehood. The manifold attractions of Connie Stuart made her an ideal wife to have at his side when he mounted the steps of the governor's mansion in Helena.

It was good to have ambition, he thought, and to make it come true all he had to do was win Connie by disposing of Captain Walt Ridgeway, who, if left free to meddle, could become a thorn in his side.

TWELVE

Larry Grimes had come to Elkhill for merchandise and sat idly on a barrel at the side of the emporium while waiting for Basil Deepcut, the storeman, to work his way through Connie Stuart's list of requirements. Her father had always taken a dim view of the use of liquor during working hours, and Larry believed the daughter would share that opinion, so quenching his thirst with a cold beer was out of the question. Instead, he'd bought a nickel's worth of jelly beans that Mrs Deepcut had supplied in a paper twist and he now sat sucking them. However, satisfying his sweet tooth did little to ease his troubled mind.

Gold had entrapped him, had forced him to remain silent while Rex Coulter had lied to Ezra Stuart and his daughter. Those lies had got the old man killed and could have ill consequences for Captain Ridgeway. He knew he should tell Miss Connie the truth, let her know that Rex Coulter had deceived her and that her former husband-to-be had done nothing more than defend himself and the Edmond girl from an unprovoked attack. But he had his colleagues to think about, too. To spill the beans about the gold in the river would put an end to their illegal prospecting and the riches they were hoping to discover.

It was the word 'gold', however, that roused him from his reverie. Sheriff Hayes, in conversation with Judge Hawkins, had paused on the front veranda to strike a match against a post in order to light up the slim cigarillo that hung between his lips.

'And this business of panning the river for gold,' Samuel Hawkins said, 'have you followed that up?'

Andy Hayes blew smoke into the air. 'Charlie Ute hasn't been around to question, and I reckon it'll be a long time before he returns to Elkhill. I spoke to Rex Coulter last night. I didn't learn anything, but he's a different man these days, belligerent and cocky, like he knows something that makes him wiser than everyone else.'

'But not the identities of the gold seekers.'

Sheriff Hayes shook his head. 'But he wasn't surprised when I told him that those doing it were wasting their time.'

'According to Captain Ridgeway,' pointed out Samuel Hawkins, as though implying some element of doubt.

'He led the surveyors' army escort,' Andy Hayes announced with firmness. 'He won't be mistaken.'

The judge conceded that history was on the soldier's side. 'No one ever found gold around here in the past.'

The two men walked on, leaving the unnoticed Larry Grimes seething in the side alley. Although he couldn't figure out the reason for the foreman's deception, it was now clear to Larry that he and the other hands had been tricked into aiding Rex Coulter for some purpose of his own. From inside the store, Basil Deepcut shouted for him, making him aware that his purchases were ready for loading on the wagon. There would be a reckoning, he vowed, when he got back to High Hill and spread his news to the rest of the men.

The sheriff and the judge were still in conversation as they drew close to the hotel, but ceased their chatter when they saw Walt Ridgeway on the veranda. He was carrying his rifle in one hand and his war-bag in the other. Despite his attempts to hide the discomfort he suffered with every movement, his hesitant, restricted strides could not disguise the damage that had been caused. Nor could the cuts and bruises that showed on his face.

'What happened to you?' Andy Hayes wanted to know.

'Connie Stuart called off the wedding and some of her crew wanted to be sure that I understood that her decision was final.'

Judge Hawkins looked pointedly at the bag in Walt's hand. 'So you're quitting town.'

'I've got a message to deliver first, but no reason to stay here after that.'

'Heading back to Fort Bridger?' asked Sheriff Hayes.

Walt finished tying his bag to the saddle-horn and slid his rifle into the holder: 'I'll be helping out at the Edmonds' place for a few days. Cassie's crew are busy out at the line camp so I'll do what I can to repair the damage to the house before I move on.' He nodded a farewell to the two men, climbed on to the bay, and rode slowly down the street towards Jonathan Barclay's office.

When the last sack of flour had been checked against the inventory and heaved into the wagon, Larry Grimes was ready for the return trip. As he gathered up the reins to urge the team forwards, two horsemen rode hurriedly past the alley opening. One of the men was Rex Coulter, and Larry's ire was instantly re-aroused. He leapt down from the wagon and re-tethered the team. Although he knew he should speak to the sheriff and let the law investigate the motives behind the foreman's lies, he was still a cowman and would give Rex the opportunity to explain matters first.

Stepping out of the alley, he'd expected to see the two riders dismounting outside the Running Steer or heading further down the street towards Reno's Retreat, but he was wrong on both counts. He didn't immediately spot the horses, which had been hitched to a rail on the other side of the street, steam rising from their bodies as though they'd been ridden to the utmost of their ability, and it took several more seconds before he caught sight of Rex Coulter and his companion. The other man was a stranger to Larry, but as the pair slipped between buildings on the far side of the street, his demeanour was no less furtive than the foreman's. His simmering anger now tempered by curiosity, Larry hurried to follow them.

Larry Grimes paused and peered cautiously into the gap between the buildings into which his prey had disappeared. The building he was leaning against was the lawyer's office, separated from a milliner's shop by a gap insufficient to admit a wagon. Larry couldn't conceive any reason for Rex Coulter visiting either of those establishments, especially via their back entrances, so he figured his destination was one of the store-houses behind. The coincidence of the lawyer's visit to High Hill that morning stirred momentarily in his mind, but he had no reason to suppose any connection existed between Jonathan Barclay and Rex Coulter. It came as surprise, therefore, as he reached the point between the buildings where the gap widened substantially, to glimpse the foreman through a window. The room he was in could only be a back room of the lawyer's office. Pressing himself tightly against the wall, Larry removed his hat in order to observe the meeting within.

Johnny Brassil was handing over a long envelope to Jonathan Barclay. The voices of the men passed thinly to Larry's ears, but he distinctly heard the lawyer ask if everyone was dead.

'All of them,' Johnny Brassil told him, words that were corroborated by Rex Coulter's mirthless grin.

125

His expression changed, however, when their attention was grabbed by a sound from beyond the window. All eyes turned in that direction, aware that any witness to their meeting could ruin their plans. Larry, who had stumbled when he'd trod upon a loose stone, had been quick enough to get his head below the level of the window, but even so, he knew he wasn't out of danger. If those inside chose to investigate the noise he would have little chance of escaping their notice. Before he could get back to the main street the door would be thrown open and his presence disclosed.

Instead of returning the way he'd come, Larry moved further into the alley. A pile of rubbish, a broken barrel and rotting planks topped with discarded rugs offered a hiding place. They promised nothing more than a slim chance of evading discovery but there was no alternative. He threw himself behind the timber, lay flat on the ground and listened for the sounds of search.

Indeed, Rex Coulter was on the point of investigating the disturbance, but another event suddenly took precedence. From the front office the sound of the street door opening reached them and the voice that called out the lawyer's name was immediately recognizable.

Rex Coulter kept his voice low. 'It's the soldier-boy. What does he want?'

'Keep quiet and wait here,' Jonathan Barclay told the others then went into the front room. 'Mr Ridgeway,' he said, greeting Walt with a broad smile and with an expansive gesture indicated the chair for visitors and asked, 'How can I help you?'

Walt waved away the proffered seat. 'I'm just here to deliver a message,' he said. 'Miss Edmond isn't interested in selling her land. There's no need for you to ride out to her place in the morning.'

'Miss Edmond is making a mistake,' the lawyer said, the smile gone from his face. 'She'll not get a better offer.'

'She doesn't want any offer at all. Like I said, she's not selling. Her situation might change, and when it does she'll look for a buyer, but her father has recently been killed and this is the wrong time for her to consider moving.'

'Perhaps I should have done more to convince her that she'd be better off among the society of a big town. A lonely ranch is no place for a girl on her own.'

'She isn't on her own. She's got a capable crew who'll keep the ranch running until she decides her future.'

'She's letting them take advantage of the situation. They'll rob her of every cent of profit while pretending to help. When I come out tomorrow I'll make her see reason. She should snap up the offer that's been made and rid herself of all these troubles.'

'I've told you, Miss Edmond doesn't want you out there tomorrow. Stay away.'

'Who gave you the right to speak with such authority?'

'Miss Edmond. I'll be doing some work for her for

the next few days and I'll be at her ranch tomorrow.'

The inference that he wouldn't allow Cassie to be further pestered hung in the air but the lawyer wasn't given the opportunity to respond. Walt had had the final word and left the office with Jonathan Barclay's eyes boring into his back.

From his hiding place in the alley, Larry Grimes saw Walt Ridgeway walk past the opening at the end of the alley aware that he'd just left the lawyer's office. Moments later, its rear door opened and Rex Coulter and Johnny Brassil emerged. Before they'd taken a step down the alley, Jonathan Barclay appeared and spoke softly and urgently to them. His face registered his black mood. 'You heard him. He must be on his way to the ranch now. Make sure he doesn't get there. Make sure he doesn't interfere with our plans again.'

Larry waited until the alley was empty before leaving his hiding place and carefully merging with those townspeople who were abroad on the main street. The horses that Rex Coulter and his friend had earlier hitched to the rail outside the lawyer's office were now gone. Larry could see them being ridden out of town at an easy canter. Next, he scanned the street hoping to catch sight of Walt Ridgeway, for he now knew that the soldier was the object of their mission. But he searched in vain. He recalled Jonathan Barclay's instruction to Rex Coulter, that he must stop the soldier reaching the ranch, and Larry had no reason to suppose that the lawyer had meant any other place than High Hill, to which they all had connections.

Walt Ridgeway had become an abomination to Connie Stuart, which rendered him an outcast to every High Hill rider, but Larry's new-found anger towards Rex Coulter was the far greater emotion. The foreman had tricked him and his bunkhouse friends with devastating results for others, and in Larry's mind he couldn't be allowed to kill the soldier who had come to Elkhill to marry his new employer. He knew that all of Captain Ridgeway's actions had been taken to defend himself or others since arriving in the territory. Now, unknown to him, men were determined to kill him. Whatever risk he posed to the fulfilment of the plans of Jonathan Barclay and his cohorts, they were ruthless enough to kill him to ensure their success. He wasn't sure how he would achieve it, but Larry was determined to foil his foreman's efforts.

He hurried back to the loaded wagon outside Basil Deepcut's store and set the team off at a brisk pace in pursuit. Towing a heavy load gave him little hope of catching the riders ahead, but he had to try. As he drove he mulled over in his mind the notion that he had another mission in addition to preventing the murder of Walt Ridgeway: Connie Stuart needed to be told the truth.

The startled people of Elkhill were drawn as if by a magnet when a man driving a buckboard arrived in town. A team of six horses trailed behind, bodies slung over some of them. The buzz of voices and bustling activity soon grabbed the attention of Andy Hayes, who joined the throng on the boardwalk. He recognized the buckboard driver as the owner of one of the smaller spreads across the river.

'What's happened, Garfield?' he asked.

'Came across the stagecoach all busted up on the other side of the river.'

'Accident?'

'Reckon it was being chased.'

'A hold-up?'

'Reckon so,' came the reply. 'I've got four dead people with me and more than one has been ventilated with lead. I would have left them out there, but the driver's still alive so I brung 'em all to town.'

'Did he say who did it?'

'Hasn't said anything. He's been unconscious all the way. He's in a bad way, sheriff.'

'Will he survive?'

'Doctor Cairns'll be able to answer that better than me. I reckon the quicker he gets a look at him the better his chances will be.'

Murmurs of agreement greeted those words, and a young lad was sent to fetch the medic. Four bystanders took it upon themselves to lift the still unconscious driver off the back of Garfield's wagon and carry him into the nearby hotel. One of them said, 'It's Buckskin,' before they disappeared indoors. Meanwhile, a handler from the coach line came to claim the horses and was told to leave the bodies draped across their backs with the undertaker.

One or two men lingered on the boardwalk to learn the sheriff's response to another hold-up, wondering if he planned to organize a posse to set off in pursuit of the killers. The lawman, however, remained silent, kept his thoughts concealed, hoping that the wounded man would survive and be able to identify the bandits who'd attacked the coach.

Mort Davis, who was the coach line operator in Elkhill, wondered aloud why that coach had been attacked.

'It wasn't carrying a strong-box,' he announced, information that was meant primarily for Andy Hayes, but was overheard by all those who were near at hand.

Garfield had brought with him the mailbags that had been in the footwell alongside the wounded driver. 'Luggage was still atop the coach,' he said, 'so I guess the robbers were content to take the money and jewellery they found on the passengers.'

No one argued, and soon the people began to disperse.

THIRTEEN

During his spell as a cadet at West Point, Walt Ridgeway had been required to attend lectures on several subjects beyond the scope of military history, tactics and discipline. Among them had been geology, a subject for which, at that time, he'd been unable to generate any enthusiasm. So although he'd acquired a basic understanding of rock formations, strata and the effects of pressure and water below the earth's surface, his knowledge was little greater than that of most men. He recognized different types of rock, knew the grey obsidian stone used by the tribespeople for tools and weapons, but couldn't identify areas that were likely to produce gold or silver deposits. Prospecting for those metals had never been an option for him.

He had, however, commanded a military escort for a party of surveyors, and his natural curiosity had broadened his knowledge. And now, as he kicked at the earth, he remembered the grin on the face of a geologist who had uncovered similar pinkish/orange soil below the surface.

'Native copper,' the man had told Walt. 'There's no gold around here, but I suspect there's a vast fortune to be made from other minerals in these hills.'

After leaving Elkhill, Walt had chosen to take the long route back to Cassie Edmond's home. The reason for the attack on her father remained a puzzle, so he'd followed the river route, drawn to the vicinity of the shooting as though a yet unnoticed clue was waiting to be discovered. He was nearing the point where he'd crossed the river when he'd lifted his eyes to the hills on his left. The sun was hot and high and brightened the colours of the tree leaves and ground flora. In addition, it seemed as though the high ground itself gleamed, emitting a kind of light that demanded investigation.

Even as he rode up the hillside, the memory of those surveyors he'd guided into other hills filled his mind. As soon as he dismounted he kicked away the top surface and looked down upon the soil revealed below. He reminded himself that he wasn't an expert, that perhaps the colours he saw were different to those that had excited the geologist, but his gut feeling told him he was right. This land, Cassie Edmond's land, was rich in copper, and someone had killed her father to get it.

If he hadn't sunk to his knees at that moment in order to scoop up a handful of soil, the bullet that whistled a foot above his head would surely have killed him. Another followed close behind but Walt flung himself to his right and began rolling across the ground, seeking the protection of one of the nearby tall ponderosa pines. Bullets chipped at the trunk, sending splinters and pieces of bark flying through the air.

Walt drew his pistol, sought the tell-tale wisps of smoke, and sent two shots in that direction. The shots that answered came from a different direction. A second gunman held a position further to the right, reducing the value of the tree as a protective shield. Walt's position was precarious. He couldn't stay where he was, but if he moved to his left he became an easier target for the first shooter. At that moment, both gunmen opened fire as if to emphasize the fact that he was caught in a cross-fire. Bullets struck the tree and, more threateningly, the ground close to where he lay.

There were more trees at his back, a denser group, which, if he could reach them, might provide a better opportunity of eluding his would-be killers. Getting to them, however, would not be an easy matter. They were uphill of his current position and could only be gained by breaking cover. At the moment, even rising to his knees put him in mortal danger. He raised his head and drew two shots from the second gunman. From the sound, it was clear that his adversaries were armed with rifles, while he had only his six-gun. His ammunition was limited, too. He travelled with the hammer on an empty chamber, and he'd used two of the five bullets, so he had only three shells in the revolver and perhaps a dozen in the loops of his gunbelt.

The guns had fallen silent. Walt listened for other sounds, the tell-tale signs that the men were moving to fresh positions in order to trap him or to find a spot that made him a clearer target. Whoever they were, he knew he couldn't remain prone any longer. He glanced behind once more, judged his best course to the tree line, then took a deep breath. To keep the second gunman's head down, he fired two shots at the place where he was concealed, then broke cover and headed uphill in a crouched run. If his calculations were correct, if the gunmen hadn't found fresh stations from which to attack his position, the tree he'd been using would still be an obstacle to a clear shot for the first shooter.

It wasn't easy running uphill while bent and trying to zig-zag to make himself a more difficult target. At any moment a bullet could end his life, and he'd hardly covered a quarter of the distance when the crack of rifle fire carried to him. Two bullets, one flying over his head and the second over his left shoulder, smacked against the trees that he hoped were his sanctuary.

The second rifle opened up and a bullet struck a snapped branch and lifted it off the ground to strike Walt's legs. He stumbled, fell, rolled, then scrambled to the foot of the nearest tree where he fired the last bullet in his gun.

A yell carried to him. He didn't think the bullet had found a mark, though it had, perhaps, been close enough to alarm one of the gunmen. He didn't stop. Again he put his faith in the thick trunk of a ponderosa pine for protection and went deeper among the trees. The gunfire behind became more intense. Bullets whistled before smacking into trees that interrupted their flight, snapping off twigs and ripping away splinters. Numerous ricochets buzzed, but none proved dangerous to Walt. When the gunfire ceased he rested his back against a wide tree and drew breath.

He listened for sounds of pursuit, figured his attackers would split up, try to catch him in a pincer movement, but knew they would be approaching with care. While they were two against his one the odds were in their favour, and it was an advantage they wouldn't want to lose. Rapidly, he emptied the spent shells from his gun and fully refilled the chambers from his belt. When he'd finished, only one loop contained a shell. If he was to overpower his attackers it had to be done swiftly.

Because he was close to the summit of the high hill, Walt deemed there was little point in climbing higher. The nearer the top they climbed the closer his adversaries would be to each other. He judged his best chance of success would be to tackle them separately. Cautiously, keeping low, he moved to his right, in the direction he assumed the second gunman would be approaching.

A sound downhill brought him to a standstill. A grunt reached him, as though someone had stubbed their toe or bumped their head. He looked for movement, but at first couldn't see anything. He stepped to the side, peered around a tree to gain a view that had been previously obscured. It was a long moment before a movement caught his eye.

The man was a stranger to Walt. He was heavy-set, his face grubby with dark stubble, and he wore dark clothes which provided adequate camouflage when he stuck to the shadows thrown by the high trees. But for two steps he was in sunlight and the rifle in his hands glinted as he stepped forwards. Walt remained motionless until, once more, they were masked from each other by trees. He'd taken note of the other's line of ascent, however, and when he did move he eased further to his right, thereby foiling their pincer movement by having both men to his left.

Almost two minutes passed before the man he'd espied further downhill appeared again. He'd reached the tree against which Walt had rested, and was now looking down at the discarded shells. He looked uphill, an expression on his face that mirrored his belief that his quarry had fled in that direction and would soon be within his rifle sights. He hefted the gun, then began his pursuit.

Before he'd taken two steps, Walt let him know he had him covered. He stepped forwards into a spot where the short distance between them was not interrupted by trees. 'Hey,' he said, barely loud enough to carry to the other, but bearing an unmistakeable threat.

Johnny Brassil turned his shoulders, saw the man he was intent upon killing but also saw the pistol in his hand. His hands twisted the rifle he was holding, bringing the barrel into line with Walt's body. His finger was within the trigger guard, but he wasn't quick enough to put it to use. Walt fired first, the bullet ripping into Johnny Brassil's belly, doubling him over, his eyes bulging. If he had any thoughts of renewing his attempt to shoot Walt they were eliminated by the soldier's second bullet, which left him dead on the ground.

Wherever he was, Walt knew that the second gunman couldn't have failed to hear the crack of gunfire. He figured he would know that only one gun had been fired, a revolver not a rifle, and as a result would draw the appropriate conclusion. He would be coming to investigate, but was unlikely to be as easily surprised as his companion had been. Even so, Walt had little option other than to lay a similar trap to the one he'd set for Johnny Brassil. Whether his remaining attacker was uphill or downhill of Walt's current situation was impossible to know. All he could do was remain alert for any sound or movement that signalled his approach.

Rex Coulter had been less than fifty yards away when the two reports had reached his ears. The lack of rifle fire put him instantly on guard and he considered his next move. If Johnny Brassil was dead then he had to face the soldier alone. Coulter liked other people around him when there was fighting to be done, but if he wanted to make a profit from the scheme he was embroiled in, then he couldn't retreat now. He tried to assess Walt Ridgeway's next move. Was he re-tracing his tracks back to his horse to make his escape, or was he lying in wait to kill again?

In Rex's opinion, the soldier's least likely course of action would be to go higher up the hill. There was nothing to be gained from such a move. If he'd intended fleeing without any more conflict he would seek out his horse and ride away. If he was planning a showdown he would be waiting somewhere in the vicinity of the man he'd slain. So Rex chose the high ground, climbing and circling until he was sure he was above the place from whence the gunshots had come. He saw Johnny Brassil's body stretched out and still. There was no doubting the fact that he was dead. He paused, hoping to hear the sound of hoof-beats. Hearing none, he concluded that Walt Ridgeway was somewhere close at hand, and he couldn't leave this hillside until he'd killed him.

Stealthily and via an indirect route, Rex descended, nervously scanning his surroundings, pausing from time to time to examine those shadows that might conceal his prey, or his hunter. He was kneeling beside a tree about ten feet above the corpse when he felt the cold barrel of a gun pressed against the back of his neck.

'Stand up,' Walt Ridgeway ordered. When he'd recognized Rex Coulter as his assailant Walt's prime thought was to discover the motive for trying to kill him. Could it be that Rex's regard for his dead employer was so great that he was prepared to commit murder to avenge his death?

Before posing any questions he had first to disarm

him. 'Tightly grip the barrel of your rifle with your right hand while you unbuckle your gunbelt with your left.'

Walt waited until Rex had complied before speaking again. Taking a couple of backward steps he began to say, 'Put them on the ground,' but before he'd completed the command his heel struck a root of the tree and he stumbled. He didn't fall, but the momentary distraction provided Rex Coulter with an opportunity to strike out.

Already the gunbelt had been dropped, but the High Hill foreman still grasped the rifle near the spout of the barrel. Seizing the moment, and swinging the gun in a powerful arc, he attempted to smash the stock against his opponent's body. Success would undoubtedly provide him with sufficient time to turn the gun in his hands and pump lead into the soldier.

Although he'd tottered and his foot had twisted slightly as he tried to regain his balance, Walt Ridgeway was still alert to the dangers of the situation. He recognized Rex Coulter's intention before the swinging rifle was halfway through its arc and could have shot him before it was completed, but he didn't yet want the man dead. First, there were questions to ask. He swayed back, putting his body out of reach of the clubbing weapon, avoiding further injury at the hands of the High Hill man.

Even so, Rex Coulter did gain some advantage from his attack. Although his swinging rifle failed to make contact with Walt's body, it clipped his revolver, knocking it from his grasp and sending it sliding across the ground into the undergrowth. Walt grunted with surprise and pain as his hand was jarred by the impact. Still, he leapt forward and barged his full weight against the other man. It was imperative that he prevented Rex from reversing his grip on the gun – failure would greatly reduce his chances of survival.

As it was, the injuries he was already carrying were a handicap to him in the current situation. Each collision of their bodies as they struggled for supremacy stirred up every small agony that had previously been inflicted by the High Hill hands. And Rex Coulter was a tough opponent. He squirmed and struggled, used knees, elbows and head in a desperate attempt to get free from the bear-like hug in which he found himself. The rifle was still secure in his hands but trapped between the two men as they rolled on the hard ground. The contest was proving to be a stalemate – Rex had the weapon but was unable to use it because of the grip in which he was held, and Walt would be risking all if he relaxed the grip on his opponent in order to disarm him.

The resolution to the problem came unexpectedly. Rex had almost gained the upper hand. His knees were on the ground either side of Walt and he was trying to prise himself and the gun away from the other's grasp. Walt's arms were tiring with the strain, and he knew that his hold would soon be broken. Summoning his strength he heaved upwards and Rex was flung aside. The foreman's head crunched against a pine tree and he was momentarily dazed.

141

The rifle began to slip from his grasp, and before he could recover his hold Walt clenched a handful of his shirt and jabbed his head against the tree once more.

Although stunned, it still wasn't easy for Walt to wrest the weapon from Rex's grip. When it did come free it was the result of a sudden jerk which sent it flying through the air and over the side of a precipice to which they'd rolled close. On hands and knees, Rex scurried after it, hoping the drop wasn't sheer and that the gun was lying within reach. It wasn't, but in any case, Walt's fist struck him in the side, driving the air out of his lungs.

Walt scrambled to his feet, the multitude of pains momentarily forgotten because of his success. 'Get up,' he said.

Rex Coulter groaned as though any movement was beyond his capacity. But it was a ruse. Lying on the ground he swung a leg, scything Walt's from under him and sending him, too, tumbling over the precipice. Rex peered over and saw his opponent face down, spread-eagled thirty feet below. He collected his gunbelt, mounted his horse and rode for Elkhill.

Walt Ridgeway wasn't dead, his descent having been more of a sliding tumble than a plummet, yet when he regained his senses, he wasn't sure that death was too far distant. Still, he knew he couldn't remain on the hillside, and made his way back to his horse. It was a slow business, as was the journey to Cassie Edmond's home.

Cassie saw his distress before he reached the ranch house, and although he was able to find a grin for her, the twisted manner in which he sat astride his horse testified to the hurt he was enduring. She helped him into the house, sat him in a chair and collected her balms and potions with which to treat him.

'Whatever you do,' he said while she bathed his cuts, 'you mustn't sell this property yet.'

Although curious, Cassie didn't speak. Instead, she kept her attention fixed on the task at hand. Soothing his pains was her prime concern – and besides, she knew he would tell her more.

'I'm not an expert,' he began, but had to stop in order to draw breath when stung by the potion she was rubbing into a shoulder abrasion.

'Sorry,' she said.

He smiled at her. 'Don't be,' he told her. 'Nobody could be gentler.'

Their eyes met. Cassie wanted to tell him that she would like always to be the one who eased his sores, but was afraid of being considered forward, or worse. She lowered her eyes to re-examine the scrape she was treating.

'I'm not an expert,' Walt began again, 'but it's possible that your land is rich in minerals. Copper, I think. I've seen soil like that in the high ground before. If I'm right you'll be a very wealthy young woman.'

Cassie wasn't sure if he was serious or teasing her.

'You'll have to have samples tested, of course, and

I would recommend you do that as soon as possible, but don't let anyone hustle you into selling until you've had the results.' He shrugged his shirt into place and began to fasten the buttons.

'There's stew in the pot if you're hungry,' said Cassie.

Walt said, 'You know what this means, don't you, Cassie?'

She paused, waited for him to continue.

'Someone else might have realized the wealth that is lying in those hills. Your father might have been killed to get their hands on this ranch.'

Cassie sat down, mention of her father's death bringing back memories of the violence visited upon the house that night.

'The lawyer who came with an offer, did he tell you who he represented?'

'No. Said it was a good offer and that I should accept it quickly before it was withdrawn.'

'Perhaps we should go into town and talk with Jonathan Barclay,' said Walt.

FOURTEEN

Larry Grimes was still half-a-dozen miles from the High Hill ranch house when he passed his employer heading in the opposite direction. Connie Stuart was sitting primly in her buggy, dressed in town clothes and driving her two-horse team at a fast run. Judging it to be an inappropriate moment to tell her about Rex Coulter's lies and intrigue, he pulled aside to let her pass. Watching her swirling dust he reached the troubling conclusion that Walt Ridgeway was not on the trail ahead, so if the High Hill ranch hadn't been the soldier's destination when he left Elkhill, then his own chances of preventing the murder were scuttled. He drove on towards the ranch with his wagon-load of goods, unsure of his next move.

Jonathan Barclay saw Connie Stuart drive into town and hitch her rig outside the hotel. He noted the smart clothes that accentuated her trim figure, and watched with much pleasure her feminine movements as she descended from the buggy and went inside. For a few moments he remained gazing out of the window, the benefits of taking Connie Stuart for his wife renewed in his head. They were still there when, a minute later, Connie walked into his office. If her arrival was unexpected, he would have been even more surprised if he'd known that it was thoughts of marriage that had brought her calling.

Ever since his visit to her home, his suitability as a suitor had lurked in her mind. Her father's death had piled a burden on her shoulders which she knew she couldn't carry alone. Ranching was in her blood, and for a while, with the assistance of her most trusted crew members, she could manage High Hill's affairs, but physically, she knew she wasn't capable of dedicating those hours of riding and labour necessary to maintain her legacy in like manner to her father. If she meant to keep the ranch, then she needed a partner who would work alongside her. It might have been different if her marriage to Walt Ridgeway had gone ahead as planned, but he had lost all favour in her eyes, and she could only now wonder what talent she thought he had possessed that had made her consider him a suitable husband.

Perhaps she'd been swayed by the uniform, or the blissful life of an army officer's wife such as had been portrayed by her friend during the visit to Fort Collins, but Jane and her husband were now in some dusty fort in the South-West Territories and Connie knew she had no desire ever to leave the lush Montana country in which she'd been reared. She'd tried to convince herself that she could be a dutiful army wife, but now, when such devotion was not required, she was honest enough to admit that it had always been her intention to persuade Walt Ridgeway to abandon his military career. He was intelligent, and with her father's guidance, could learn to manage cows and men as he had horses and soldiers in the cavalry. That scheme had been brutally brought to an end. Now another was growing in her mind.

Like Walt Ridgeway, Jonathan Barclay wasn't a cattleman, but as with the soldier, Connie believed that if the running of High Hill became his responsibility he could be moulded into a capable manager and partner. He had, of course, his own legal office to maintain, but she saw in him a man of ambition who would be happy to spread his wings, and take on new challenges that would increase his authority and influence throughout the area. She tried to keep the word 'power' out of her inner deliberations, but power, she guessed when she thought of the greedy light that filled his eyes when he'd looked at her, was what he wanted, and powerful he would be if he became master at High Hill.

Of course, marriage wasn't as cut and dried as a business relationship. She would need to know that they could live together at least in pleasant companionship, if not love. So she'd come to talk to him, to ask him to act on her behalf by informing the various associations of which her father had been a member of his death. And as she had taken a room at the hotel for an overnight stay, she also asked if perhaps he would join her there for dinner.

'I can't think of anything that would give me more pleasure,' he told her.

'My father was a rancher of the old school,' she said, 'here before there was law of any kind, so he was accustomed to handling his problems personally. I wondered in what capacity he'd used your services?'

Jonathan Barclay uttered some glib phrases. 'It's true that your father saw little need for law books and legal deeds when I first arrived in Elkhill. He was a tough man whose personal history was told by every look in his eye, every line on his face and every move-ment he made. But he was never one of those who dismissed my practice or deemed lawyers and judges worthless among these remote communities. He was clear in his thinking about the future. Realized that one day every dispute would be settled in a court of law, not by the man who wielded the greater fire-power.'

Connie smiled, nodded her head in acknowledge-ment of Jonathan Barclay's homilies, then tilted her head for him to continue, to answer the question she'd asked.

'He first came to me to document a settlement he'd reached with Peterkins over timber rights on your northern boundary. After that I endorsed bills of sale for cattle he sold to some Wyoming buyers. Small registrations that would avoid future disputes. I didn't do a lot of work for your father, but his need of my services was beginning to increase, and I regarded him as much as a friend as I did a client.'

He offered her one of his most charming smiles. 'I hope that our relationship, too, will be more friendship than client.'

'Perhaps that's something we can discuss over tonight's meal,' she replied. 'Shall we say eight o'clock?'

'I can barely wait,' he said, as they both stood and he began to escort her to the street door.

Before they reached it, the door from the rear room was thrust open and Rex Coulter rushed into the office. Grass still clung to his clothing, his hair was awry, and the urgency that had caused such an entrance was marked by the wild-eyed expression on his face. At this hour, when the business day was drawing to a close, he had assumed that the lawyer would be alone and his initial view of the room confirmed that expectation. Connie Stuart's trim form was obscured from his view by the lawyer's larger body.

'It's done,' he said. 'He's dead.'

He'd spoken with gusto, confident that such tidings would be greeted with enthusiasm by the other man. He was stopped in his tracks, however, by the glare that was turned upon him and his mouth sagged when he realized that the lawyer was not alone. His discomfort increased when he identified Jonathan Barclay's visitor.

'Who is dead?' Connie Stuart wanted to know.

Rex Coulter made a silent appeal for help to Jonathan Barclay.

'What's going on?' she asked, prepared to listen to

149

an answer from either man. When there was no immediate response, she fixed her attention on her foreman. 'What are you doing here?'

It was Jonathan Barclay, of course, who spoke, his mind working quickly, contriving a story to appease her curiosity. 'Connie,' he said, 'sit down, please.'

The familiarity of his address pricked Rex Coulter. His plans would be shattered by any liaison between his boss and the lawyer. His hoped-for influence as top man at High Hill would be shattered forever. For the moment, though, he didn't interrupt Jonathan Barclay's speech.

'I wasn't quite truthful with you about my dealings with your father. Brad Edmond was in financial difficulties and was prepared to sell out to your father. I drew up the necessary documents which both parties signed in this office. I was holding them here until I had the opportunity to take them through to the state office in Helena for ratification. When that was completed your father would pay the money and the Edmonds would vacate the land. In the meantime, however, Brad Edmond discovered that there were mineral deposits in the high ground which increased the value of the land. He tried to renege on the deal, and when your father wouldn't renegotiate he had someone break into this office and steal the documents. That's what the fight was about out at the Edmond ranch. Your father went there to discuss the matter, get back the document, but Brad Edmond opened fire.'

'But Brad Edmond was shot by the river.'

'That's the story put about by the Edmond girl, her Ute ally and, I'm sorry to say, your ex-fiancé to cover their own part in that deadly affray. Unfortunately, at the moment we are unable to disprove their statements to get you the justice you deserve.'

Connie dwelt on the lawyer's words for a moment, words which were in accordance with her own convictions and therefore had to be true. 'So who is dead?' she asked, referring to the words blurted out by her foreman when he'd stormed into the room.

Again it was Jonathan Barclay who spoke. 'Walt Ridgeway,' he said, pausing a moment to let the young woman ingest the victim's identity. 'On your behalf,' he continued, 'I have tried to re-open negotiations with Brad Edmond's daughter. I told her I'd be there tomorrow morning with a bid that she would find acceptable, but Walt Ridgeway was here earlier threatening me to stay away. It seems he'd set himself up as the girl's protector or, perhaps, he has plans himself for the wealth that is in the hills. I asked Rex to speak with him, to try to dissuade him from interfering, but I guess he didn't take the advice too kindly.'

Connie turned her gaze on Rex Coulter for confirmation.

'He went for his gun,' the foreman said. 'I was just too quick for him.'

'Rex was very loyal to your father,' Jonathan Barclay said. 'I knew I could depend on his assistance.'

'And you intend to get the land from Cassie Edmond?' Connie asked him.

'I do.'

She stood. 'I'll expect you at eight,' she said, then left the office.

'Do you think she believed that?' asked Rex Coulter.

'She wants to believe it, so even if there are things that don't seem right to her, she's not going to dispute them.'

'What about the Edmond ranch – you made her think you were buying it for her.'

'Yeah! Well perhaps I am. A wedding present that will make us the richest couple in Montana.'

'I thought that might be your plan.' Rex's tone was surly.

Jonathan Barclay laughed. 'Had notions in that direction yourself, did you?' When Rex refused to answer he asked, 'Where's Johnny Brassil?'

'Dead. The soldier boy killed him.'

The lawyer grunted, not dismayed – Johnny Brassil was Fred Winterfield's man, nothing to him. 'And you're sure that Ridgeway is dead?'

'Fell over a hill. Last I saw of him he was spread out a long way below.'

It wasn't much more than an hour later when Larry Grimes returned to Elkhill. If Walt Ridgeway had been killed, then news of it would spread around the town like wildfire. He made the Running Steer his destination, but before he reached it he crossed paths with Connie Stuart who had been to the home of the seamstress who made her dresses. Larry lifted his hat and gripped it with both hands against his chest, plucking up the courage to tell her the things he thought she ought to know.

'Miss Stuart,' he began, 'there are things I need to tell you.'

Connie Stuart had stopped when Larry addressed her, but not to pay attention to his words. Her gaze had fixed on the horseman riding slowly along the street who halted and dismounted outside Jonathan Barclay's office. He moved awkwardly, jerkily, as betokens a man with multiple injuries to arms and legs. But she hadn't expected him to be moving at all, because Rex Coulter had brought the news that he was dead.

Further along the street, that man, too, had his eyes fixed on the new arrival. Rex Coulter had just left the Running Steer and was stopped in his tracks by the sight of Walt Ridgeway heading for Jonathan Barclay's office. Rex didn't know how the soldier had survived but he was determined to put an end to his persistent interference. He couldn't be allowed to ruin the scheme that would make him a rich man. He drew his revolver and fired.

The bullet missed Walt Ridgeway by inches, smacking instead into the wall of the building that housed the lawyer's office. Walt ducked and knelt beside a slim upright that supported the canopy over the boardwalk. Another bullet plucked a chunk from that same piece of timber. As Walt drew his own gun he scanned the far side of the street in order to locate his attacker. It took barely a moment to identify Rex Coulter who, confident of success with his first shot, had taken no precautions for his own safety. He stood on the edge of the boardwalk with the smoking gun in his hand.

Walt fired at him, quickly, the bullet flying wide but close enough to make the High Hill foreman seek some protection by darting to the corner of building. From the cover it provided he could take more careful aim at his enemy.

Walt knew the gunfire had aroused activity further along the street. Distant shouts reached his ears, someone issuing orders with a voice of authority. Although he guessed it was Sheriff Hayes who was trying to put a stop to the gunplay, Walt ignored the yells and kept his eyes focused on the other side of the street. If Rex Coulter meant to continue the fight, meant to make another attempt on his life, he would be ready for him.

Rex, of course, was forced to face the reality of the situation. He had launched an unprovoked attack and he would wind up in the cells if the soldier-boy was still alive to testify against him. There was an opportunity now to escape. He could flee down the side of the building and lie low until he could reach his horse and get out of town. Andy Hayes wouldn't come out to High Hill to arrest him over a couple of gunshots. His decision was made, one last look at the crouching figure across the road then he began to turn away. A commotion close at hand drew him back again, gave him hope that he would get another shot at his target before he was forced to make his escape.

Jonathan Barclay's words had stayed with Connie Stuart ever since leaving his office. Walt Ridgeway meant to deny her the land and wealth she believed were rightly hers. He'd thrown his hand against her and now he was trying to kill her foreman. She didn't know who owned the horse tethered to the nearby rail but she could see a rifle housed in the boot attached to the saddle. The post that provided minimal protection for Walt against Rex Coulter's bullets was no shield against an attack from her position. He was a clear target. She pulled the weapon free and worked its lever as she lifted it to her shoulder. So big was the target of his back that she barely needed to aim. She began to squeeze the trigger.

'No,' yelled Larry Grimes as he pushed up the barrel so that the bullet flew into the air. ''You're aiming at the wrong man,' he told her. Livid to be thwarted by the intervention of her own employee, Connie's eyes blazed with hatred, but it didn't stop Larry wresting the rifle from her grip. 'Rex Coulter lied to you just as he lied to your father. It wasn't Walt Ridgeway's fault that your father was killed. Everything happened the way he told it.'

The light of anger remained in Connie's eyes, but she didn't try to retrieve the gun because in that instant the duel between her foreman and ex-fiancé had reached its climax. In normal circumstances, men would automatically turn in the direction of an unexpected gunshot, so when Connie pulled the trigger behind Walt Ridgeway it was only natural for Rex Coulter to believe his adversary would be thrown off guard and provide him with a killing shot.

It didn't work out like that. Walt's military discipline kept him at his post. When Rex moved away slightly from the corner of the building, Walt fired. The first bullet struck Rex in the midriff, so that his body curled and twisted into an awkward arrangement of folding arms and buckling legs. The second bullet hit him in the chest and flung him back against the wall of the building behind.

Sheriff Hayes shouted again as he drew closer. 'Throw down those guns. I'll shoot the next person whose fires.'

Walt was happy to comply and dropped his revolver on to the dusty street. Larry Grimes did the same with the rifle that Connie had removed from some man's saddle boot. Rex Coulter's six-gun was on the ground, but not of his own volition.

'Is that Rex Coulter?' Andy Hayes asked when he saw the body stretched out on the far boardwalk.

'Twice today he's tried to kill me.' Walt told him.

'He's been a busy boy, because I wanted to ask him some questions about a stagecoach hold-up earlier today. The driver's regained consciousness. He recognized Coulter's voice and told me that Mr Barclay had some involvement, too.'

'Barclay,' muttered Walt, and the probability that the lawyer had been behind the events that had led to so many killings became all too obvious.

At that moment, a shout went up from one of the sheriff's deputies. 'There he is.' He was pointing down the alley which gave access to the lawyer's other exit.

From the moment Rex Coulter's first shot at Walt Ridgeway had struck the wall of his building, Jonathan Barclay had been engulfed by the suspicion that everything was beginning to fall apart. For a moment he'd considered taking an active part in the gunfight. He had the opportunity to kill Walt Ridgeway as he crouched at the foot of the post below his window, but even he would have found difficulty in providing a story that would justify back-shooting. Then it was all too late. Connie Stuart's anger was quelled by the young cowboy who'd taken the gun from her, and Rex Coulter was lying dead on the street. His only hope was to get away quickly. Ride for Wyoming or Nebraska where the law couldn't touch him.

The deputy's shout put an end to that plan. He wasn't a foolish man, wouldn't try to shoot it out with Andy Hayes and his men, would put his faith in his ability to talk himself off the gallows in a courtroom. He held up his hands and surrendered.

By the end of the week, when it was time for Walt Ridgeway to return to Fort Bridger, Jonathan Barclay's chances of escaping the hangman's noose had been greatly reduced. The letter stolen from the Territorial representative, George Turnbull, had been found in the lawyer's desk. Figuring that the

157

letter had been the reason for the hold-up led Sheriff Hayes to believe that Barclay had had advance warning of the coach on which Mr Turnbull was due to travel, which, in turn, pointed to an accomplice in Helena. Fred Winterfield was soon flushed out, and he, who could plead ignorance of the violence that had taken place around Elkhill, was willing to ease his own punishment by pointing a finger at Jonathan Barclay.

'Winterfield will still go to prison,' Andy Hayes predicted when he spoke to Walt Ridgeway, 'but Barclay will hang. Fitting,' he added, 'that a lawyer should be executed by the law, but more than that it proves our justice system is sound and boosts our case for statehood.'

Walt didn't argue, he had a more personal matter to resolve long before Montana became a state.

He'd remained at Cassie Edmond's home all week doing what he could to help around the place. The letter that George Turnbull had brought had confirmed Walt's opinion, that Cassie was going to be a very wealthy young woman.

'Don't act hastily,' he told her over dinner on their last night together. 'Get the advice of someone you can trust.'

'That would be you,' she'd told him and it was clear that she wanted him beside her, rich or poor.

The next day, as he mounted his horse for the return journey to Fort Bridger, he told Cassie he would be decommissioned in a year.

'I'll be waiting,' she told him, 'and you won't get

away from this bride when you come back to Elkhill.'

She watched until he'd ridden out of sight towards the river crossing near Eagle Pass.